AZTECS AT THE GUGGENHEIM

For Jennifer,
My new Friend! These
are for you. Other fictions
are forthcoming. Great meeting
you at the ASF in Baltimore.

STORIES BY
RICHARD GARCIA

Sincerely,
Richard Garcia
— 2011 —

ISBN: 1-4196-7617-2
ISBN-13: 9781419676178

Visit www.booksurge.com to order additional copies.

TABLE OF CONTENTS

I Saw an Aztec
at the Guggenheim

I looked at the first stone statue and thought it was too short. Life-sized, the audio tour guide said into my headphones. I noticed some small areas of stone that had broken off: a missing nose, a little toe, a chip from the shoulder. And empty fingers meant to hold a weapon. Or another Aztec. Nevertheless, I looked at this ancient stone, about a foot from my own long nose, knowing that Aztecs, or perhaps, one solitary Aztec, created this life-sized stone. I said, softly, so that only I could hear, It's them.

I looked to the right of the rotunda and noticed the Museum Café. I remembered that I'd felt hungry when I got of the 4 Train on Eighty-Something and Second Ave. Because I didn't know which way I faced as I emerged from underground, I began walking toward the Guggenheim in the wrong direction. I ultimately made a circle and found myself at the hole leading down to the train I'd just ridden. So, after I asked someone who appeared to be a New Yorker, I tried again.

It's that way. You're close.

I left the circle along the New York streets and walked through the Guggenheim entrance. In the rotunda, in front of the Museum Café, I felt hungry. I thought I'd better eat before seeing the featured Aztec exhibit. I stood behind an old White couple who appeared to be regulars. They seemed to know their way around the museum the way I know my way around my office. The wife looked up at the menu on the wall as the husband looked into the crowded dining room for a seat.

Look, Dear. They're serving Mexican food. How appropriate.

I thought there must be a word for this kind of form. A word like "onomatopoeia" that has to do with function rather than sound. I desperately wanted to intrude when the husband smiled in agreement.

This is an Aztec *exhibit; not a* Mexican *one. These people existed before the Spanish arrived in the New World— their old world. Your comment, while apt, is imprecise. I'm a Mexican; not an Aztec. I ate this food as a child; they didn't. Life exists independent of Europe, I suspect.*

I didn't say a word. I don't think they were interested in hearing me. I certainly wasn't.

In the end, the wife ordered a Caesar Salad. I don't know what the husband ordered. I do know it wasn't Aztec food. I went for the Grilled Chicken on Focaccia. The Mexican food seemed to me an anachronistic last meal before I was to meet the Aztecs.

I walked out of the café into the museum lobby into the ascending circular exhibit: gold jewelry, masks, figurines, big heads. Stone. It's where ancient Mexico's history ended.

I'd purchased the audio headphones for two reasons: I wanted a narrator to guide me through antiquity because I would have been lost in the present if left to my own interior narration. And because I didn't want to hear any tourists' comments about Mestizos, lost civilizations, pyramids, the number zero, clocks, hearts, gold, gods, ships, Cortez, or blue eyes.

The audio tour narrator described the Guggenheim display with an ending in mind. With a beginning, middle, and end in mind. I listened to the narrator and wanted to correct her: ancient Mexican history is not over. History, it seemed to me in that rotunda, ever circling upward, continues right through the present.

The future forever eludes us.

The White museum members were polite enough not to stare at me. While I couldn't hear them when the narrator talked, I did hear them during her silences. The patrons commented on the figures and figurines on display in these silences. However, since I wore a museum headdress that provided audio to my visual, I didn't catch all that my New York contemporaries had to say. Did they see me and wonder if I was a descendant of ancient Mexico? Of modern Mexico? Was I a living version of the stones they paid to see? They could have seen me for free walking around Second Ave. looking for them.

Without narration, however.

I saw others like me walking up and around the modern architectural evidence of New York civilization. The Guggenheim displays Aztecs: Live and in Stone. Get your headphones at the door. $2 off with a coupon.

The Guggenheim is a circular building, ascending to the top in tiresome circles, adorned with proof of the past. It's a place where I thought I'd go see proof that I ever existed at all. Museums do that for me. The first portrait I saw at the Norton in Pasadena was Van Gogh. More than this, I remember reading the narration beside his self-portrait. Or was that one his mother?

I developed nausea on the third floor of the Guggenheim, about half way up the exhibit. (I hesitate to label it the "third" floor, as I perceive "floors" on top of one another, like a totem pole. These "floors" were connected, one to the next, like time.)

I became dizzy.

I took a break and went into one of the classical rooms and enjoyed some Van Gogh, Pissarro, Picasso, Cezanne, et al., before regaining my balance. I lost my vertigo along the straight lines of the classical room.

I went out into the Aztec exhibit and saw an altar good for obtaining still-beating hearts with a single stroke. Sun god. Rain god. Moon god. Gods of stone who governed ancient Aztec elements and life.

I saw a brown figure high upon a pedestal with only his insides showing. The covering flesh and skin were missing. Liver, gall bladder, kidneys, spleen, lungs, and heart were suspended from above. I saw the inside of an Aztec from below. I don't remember the intestines. I couldn't help but stare at the heart of the Aztec. I imagined it beat beating before someone cut it out. Or else, maybe he was the one who would cut out another's heart. Or maybe he wasn't involved in this line of work at all.

In the distance: a serpent headdress with eagle wings whose past was within reach of my present.

I left the museum, walked downtown to the theater district and bought a half-priced ticket at TKTS in Time Square. I then walked a long way to my Greenwich Village hotel where I would rest until the play about a German transvestite living in Germany during the Nazi regime began. I walked past both New Yorkers and foreign visitors to get to my room. I was neither a New Yorker nor a foreigner. I felt older than I am. Time does not easily permit me to sense it in small distances. Only after long times—years, decades, centuries, even. But minutes, too, can be felt. Can be touched. Can manifest changes in reality that are the difference between life and death. For example, a beat beating heart cut out of a live warrior can cross from life to death in a few seconds, where eternity happens in brief time. And an Aztec can circle the Guggenheim in a couple of hours and dissolve time between antiquity and a New York afternoon over a cold sandwich and a hot cup of coffee.

TRUMPET LESSONS

Trinidad Turista was comfortable with words. He spoke with uninhibited words, free to do what they wanted. Easy, like a jazz ballad. Vignettes, little stories about stories, within stories. About everything and nothing. Trinidad Turista talked in rhythms, at times, with digressions and diminuendos, whispers of breaths and hesitations parading around and within the spoken words to tell of something more and less than the words themselves. Low, soft whispers that could barely be heard told the most about Trinidad Turista. And his pauses, too, in the absence of words or sounds, drew attention not only to themselves, but to surrounding sounds. Voids filled with notions oscillated between quick and slow and soft and loud. Slurs of circumvented words implied much more and much less than the accumulation of their meanings. Nuance, lucidity, purity. Said everything. And nothing.

I met my father only a few times before his foretold death. My mother saw him once on East Main: I'd know that walk anywhere. She stopped out of pity and nostalgia to give him a ride back to his mother's house where he had lived for many years—ever since he returned from his military service in Vietnam. I sat in the back seat and noticed only a view of his face from behind, at an angle. He looked back. I noticed his brown smile. Deep lines of sad and smile covered the fine bones of his face. I didn't recognize this father's face from anywhere in memory.

Disremembered.

My mother, at times, would tell me: Trinidad Turista taught himself to play the trumpet. He played by ear. Jazz mostly. Back and forth with the other players.

She told me about my father so that I could know who he was. And who he was not. I never hid Trinidad Turista from you. I never kept you away from him. He's an addict. That's why I never hid him from you.

I listened to Trinidad Turista talk as I sat in the back of my mother's car and thought about his absence from my life.

I said nothing.

■   ■   ■

My mother decided I should play the trumpet when I was thirteen.

Trinidad Turista played. Maybe you'll be good at it.

Later, during the heat of an early adolescent Edison summer, I sat with Trinidad Turista on the green couch in his mother's living room for the first time. I felt the tired coils beneath the crushed velvet suspending me. The house was sad and alive. The fumes of extinguished cigarette remnants and warm red wine the dull color of venous blood filled the living room.

There, in his mother's house, where I had never hoped to be alone with my father, I sat beside Trinidad Turista on the couch in such a way that he would have noticed if I tried to look at him. I looked straight ahead at the sheet of music notes he wrote for me to play with the used trumpet my mother bought. Old, dented, dull. This was the first time I had ever been left alone with my father. Naturally, I was afraid.

Give me your trumpet. Listen to me play. First a C. He flicked the bending silver ash hanging from the end of his cigarette before he put it on the edge of the coffee table facing him. Then he caressed my old trumpet with his brown finger tips stained from years of holding cigarette butts. Later, if you're any good, your mother said she would buy you a new trumpet.

My trumpet looked comfortable in his hands. Like it belonged there. He pursed his relaxed lips together and breathed into the horn. A gentle middle C emerged from the end. Trinidad Turista held the relentless note for all time. Softly, then very softly, then almost unhearable. Quiet as possible while still being sound. The note ended in eternity while he pressed his lips against the mouthpiece before the eternal note became a little louder, ascending through the softest sounds and then gradually through a less soft sound then louder, then loud until I could no longer believe he was still playing the same preternatural C. Slow, provocative in the end. I never imagined such a sound. When his breath stopped flowing through the old trumpet, I knew, with the imaginable certainty of life, I could never play the trumpet.

Hear it with your mind. That was a middle C.

I picked up the horn and breathed into the mouthpiece. With my lips pursed together, tight, so air itself had trouble escaping, I blew a breath of fear into the poor trumpet. No music emerged from the trumpet's end; but the fear of an adolescent alone with his father for the first time.

Relax your embouchure. Natural, like it belongs with the trumpet. Your mouth and the mouthpiece are one.

I tried to relax, but was too afraid. Of what, I don't know. I puckered into my mouthpiece and blew as hard as I could. But no air left my mouth until, finally, an insolent note came out of the end. Nothing my mind had heard; nothing like Trinidad Turista's note. I declined to play more.

Good. Now all you have to do is practice. Make the notes simple. Subtle. Here, I'll write some notes down and you play them.

Trinidad Turista drew some notes on the sheet of music paper and put letters and the finger combinations under each one. Try the notes in the spaces between the lines first: F-A-C-E.

First the F. Then the others. I played F-A-C-E. Then more notes. I learned the finger combinations for each note on his music scale. Within an hour I could play any note he wrote on the blank sheets. He wrote half-notes and quarter-notes and eighth-notes. He wrote combinations of notes which became sounds slurred together which became scales which became parts of songs. Flat and sharp. Trinidad Turista wrote notes and I played them. I learned to play the trumpet that day, but unlike Trinidad Turista, who never received a trumpet lesson.

My father and I differed.

Trinidad Turista slurred, Time doesn't exist in music. Not like you think. Time is the number of beats in a bar, not the speed of the music. Time is not a measure of duration, but of events. It took me a while to learn this. But you're smarter than me. Your mother did a good job raising you. I don't blame her for anything. The only thing I asked was that she let me name you Miles. But she said no. She didn't think Miles Turista would be a good name for a Mexican boy to grow up with. That's the only mistake I think she made.

■ ■ ■

I began in Beginning Band. By the second quarter the music teacher transferred me to Intermediate Band. Then Advanced Band. And by the end of the year I played First Chair in Advanced Band. I didn't like playing the trumpet. I never practiced at home. The next year I didn't register for Band. My mother demanded,

Why aren't you playing the trumpet anymore? I hate it. If you like it so much, you play. I quit.

■ ■ ■

I didn't miss having a father. I didn't think so when I was a boy. I saw Trinidad Turista a few times as I got older. Once in a liquor store. I walked over to get a twelve pack of Olympia beer while my friend waited in the parking lot. Inside the liquor store I heard a voice call out my name. I looked deeper into the liquor store to see who had called me. I only saw bottles of red wine, some pink and clear, too, that blurred the bright store. I didn't recognize anyone. I heard the voice again. Softer this time.

Oh. It's not you, he hesitated.

Then I could see him. I still didn't recognize him. Trinidad Turista looked at me and said, It's you.

As he walked toward me, my voluntary muscles tensed without my sensing them. He had an oblique bandage over the left side of his neck. Trinidad Turista noticed I was staring at his bandaged neck.

This happened when I tried to kill myself. I tried to cut my own jugular vein. The doctor said I stopped just before I cut my vocal cords. That would have been the end of my voice forever.

He had just been released from the Psychiatric Ward at the Valley Community Hospital outside of Edison.

I stared at my father's face—like mine, sort of.
Trinidad Turista looked down and up at me and realized, You're so big now. I hear you're in college.
I *went* to college. I graduated a few months ago.
Trinidad Turista said something to me in Spanish.
My friend is waiting outside. I left.

■　■　■

I didn't think much about Trinidad Turista after that night in the liquor store. I never thought of him much before then while he was alive.

Trinidad Turista
Musician
   Trinidad Turista, 52, died Tuesday at home. Born in Edison, Turista was a jazz musician. He served in the U.S. Air Force and played the trumpet with various Air Force bands in Vietnam. He played night clubs in San Francisco during the 60s and 70s and was instrumental in spreading jazz in the Valley. He is survived by two sisters and a brother. Funeral services will be held. Jazz will be played.

■　■　■

Trinidad Turista's muted half notes slurring, lingering forever in a timeless diminuendo barely audible with an ordinary ear. He lived before I was born.

A familiar man came to his house, ending my trumpet lesson during the adolescent summer the first time I sat with my unknown father. The man wore ragged, stained khakis and thick glasses with one cracked lens held together with a piece of clear tape. Oily hair straight down to his shoulders resting on a holey T-shirt.

I looked at the music sheet: F-A-C-E. I played the music my father had written for me. My lips grew tired. I didn't want to play anymore. I looked down the eternal hall and into the room where the familiar man tied something around his arm.

Trinidad Turista died as a memory. I stood at the edge of the small crowd at the cemetery outside of Edison. The grave had already been prepared. Three belts controlled by valves suspended the casket as someone talked. The talking stopped and some musicians stood up. No trumpet. A deliberate cantabile. Slow and leisurely: *adagio. Affettuoso.* Slower and broader and more dignified: *allargando. Pianissimo.* And, finally, as quiet as possible while still being sound: *pianississimo.*

A New York Jazz Club Once

I work in an office without responsibility in Edison. The details of my work don't matter here, so I won't bother you with them. Rather, I'll simply state that I wanted to leave the country for vacation. This would be my first trip out of California. For years, my friend and I talked about going to see one of the big tennis tournaments. The French Open was our first choice; but we decided on New York because it is closer, we both speak only English, and we know the rate of exchange for the US dollar there. The Edison dollar doesn't go far in New York, but I wanted to see the world, and I knew it would cost me. The US Open, then.

Jorge, the rhetorician, is a professor in a small liberal arts college outside of Chicago. We'd only seen each other three times in the past seven or eight years. The last time was when he served as the best man at my wedding. We planned to meet in New York to catch up in person. I flew from Sacramento. He flew from Chicago. We agreed to meet at the Manhattan hotel since he would land in New Jersey, and I at JFK. I called some New York friends to meet us for dinner. Jorge, the rhetorician, and these friends of mine had never met, though they'd all heard of each other—except for my Wall Street friend's model wife. I missed their wedding, and looked forward to meeting her for the first time.

Jorge, the rhetorician, and I arrived at the hotel within a couple of hours of each other. Since neither of us knew much about restaurants in Manhattan, Alejandro recommended we meet for dinner at Carmine's. He would leave Wall Street, meet his model wife, and wait for us at the bar.

Sounds good to me.

My other New York friend, a vascular surgeon from Cornell, couldn't make it for dinner, but said he'd meet us later at the jazz club. I don't know if he had an operation scheduled that would run late. Or if it was something else. He did want to get home from the hospital before meeting up with us.

We met at Carmine's, found each other at the bar, exchanged language about red wines, and tried to decide between Zin and Cab. I believe we went with a spicy Zin. We waited at the bar about an hour. I talked with the model wife while Jorge, the rhetorician, listened to Alejandro's talk about his newly acquired Latin American account. He flies to Buenos Aires and Mexico City as part of the Latin American Division. This seemed more interesting to Jorge, the rhetorician, than the usual university faculty dinner talk of metonymic devices.

I told the model wife that I'd seen pictures of her in Edison. That's how I recognized her at the bar when we arrived at Carmine's. I didn't want to simply walk up and tell her that I'd seen her in pictures. She probably gets that a lot. She sat alone while Alejandro went to the men's room, I deduced. I waited until he returned, saw him walk up to her, then made my move.

Alex. You made it. Or something like that.

We greeted each other; he introduced me to her.

I saw your wedding pictures in Edison. I thought this was you sitting alone at the bar, but couldn't be certain in this New York crowd. I didn't want to approach you alone at the bar. I could have been wrong.

I introduced them to Jorge. He's a professor of rhetoric. I'm not sure either of them knew what that meant. We exchanged language about red wines and ordered a bottle from California. I believe I urged it more than the others.

About an hour later I sat across from Alejandro while Jorge, the rhetorician, sat across from the model wife. I'm not sure what they talked about, but I noticed an intensity in their conversation I could not have expected. Did they discuss runway or prolepsis techniques?

Alex explained that buying and selling a house every 2-5 years for 30 years is a better strategy than buying one house and holding it for thirty years. I didn't quite understand how that worked; but could not imagine myself in one place for thirty years under any circumstances. So, I agreed with him.

He manages Argentina and Mexico, primarily. I suppose there are other countries in his Latin American Division. Spain, I think, was included, though I could not decipher how. It seemed more European than Latin American to me. At that time, Argentina was descending into fantastic financial dust. My reference to Borges went unheard at the New York bar.

The four of us left Carmine's and met up with the vascular surgeon on Broadway in front of the Manhattan Sheraton. After introductions, we walked to the jazz club on the next corner. His wife, also a surgeon, didn't join us that night.

Thelonious Monk's former trio played that night. We walked in the front door, down the stairs, and met the waitress. She gave us two warnings. The first: she warned that a toilet had overflowed earlier and that the seating would be toward the back for that night. The orchestra section of the little club was flooded, empty. People sat up, in the next two levels. I recognize here that this sounds like a big club, but it wasn't. Each level up was not deep. We sat in front of the others in the audience—closest to the trio on stage, but still far from them considering the intimate attempt in this small jazz club.

The front section is closed.

A plumber worked on the toilet on the other side of the wall next to the trio as they played notes of past jazz. We ordered drinks. The $20 cover charge for each of us was to be added to the final bill.

Naturally, we talked over the music, loud enough for each to hear the other. The vascular surgeon still needed to get through the introductions, how we all knew each other, and explain what he did, precisely, during his vascular dissections to a group of foreign New Yorkers—me, a rhetorician, a young Wall Street man, and his model wife—who could not imagine the obliteration of vessels inside our own, or any other, bodies.

Second: the waitress warned that this was her first night on the job. We didn't know whether to believe her; but didn't care. I did wonder why she told us that.

The jazz club appeared to be an intimate setting, alive with jazz artists and audience response. A dynamic, original art that exists only in the present.

Soon after she sat us, and before our drinks arrived, our waitress, on what was her first night, so she said, gently asked us to keep our voices down so the audience could hear the Thelonious Monk derivative trio.

We laughed and giggled like school children after the teacher had shushed us. Two professors, a Wall Street manager of the Latin American Division and his model wife, and a dreamy officemate, all whispering loudly to one, then to the other.

It's not her first night.

I hope she gets my drink right.

Did you pay at the door?

The flood isn't all that deep.

Smells bad.

My legs burn when I walk. Should I have that checked?

Where might I have seen your face?

What did you order?

I should have ordered that.

How do you two know each other?

Now I have to use the men's room. You think it's closed?

Who is Thelonious Monk?

The lead musician (bass? or piano? maybe the drummer?) spoke with the manager between songs. During the second song, on what was possibly her first night, the waitress came to us again, gently, again, and reminded us to please keep our voices down.

After the second song, the leader spoke into the microphone. I heard the drilling recreate from the men's room, and noticed a gentle rippling in the pooled toilet water on the orchestra floor. The lead spoke into the microphone. I noticed the bassist zipping his bass bag. Now I remember: the bass wasn't the lead.

We can't play under these conditions, he said.

I wondered which it was:

1. Lack of intimacy for the alive jazz trio in a small club?

2. The drilling sound in the toilet interfering with their music?

3. The toilet water pooled, stagnant and rippling on the orchestra floor, the chairs with their legs pointed upward on the table without any memory of anyone sitting there?

4. Us talking? This was the last consideration, which I instantly ruled out as impossible.

The cover charge and drinks needed to be paid, the first-time waitress informed us in a pleasant tone. Jorge, the rhetorician, informed her that we refused to pay the $20 each for entry to the underground jazz club, and that they should provide us with another free drink for our troubles since we only heard two songs. In a fit of fairness, the vascular surgeon offered to pay for the drinks. But Jorge, the rhetorician, thought the club should give us the drinks as compensation. He argued that we shouldn't pay for them, but should receive them as apologia. After all, the trio cut the show short. In either case, we certainly would not pay any cover charge.

Jorge, the rhetorician, constructed his narrative to the waitress with the manager as his intended audience. She reminded him that this was her first night, and that she had no authority to wave any charges.

We'd like your manager to explain to us why we should pay a cover charge when the trio only played two songs.

She left and returned and reported that the manager gave us half off the cover charge. So, $10 each. Plus drinks.

We refuse to pay. We'll wait to speak with the manager directly.

I couldn't know whether the manager didn't want to confront us; whether he was dealing with the trio; or the plumber. I never considered other audience members in this unknown.

By then we were all standing up, near the entrance at the base of the stairs, waiting for the manager. I noticed the door above the stairs that led down to the jazz club on 7th Avenue. I looked over the dark flight of stairs that led up. Up, onto 7th Avenue, near 51st, without signaling the others, without introduction, without ceremony or declaration, without attention, I started my climb up from underground. Up the dark stairwell from underground and onto the street in front of the door at 7th Avenue near 51st.

Police lined the street. The opening NFL football game was scheduled for the next afternoon. Bon Jovi was setting up for the pre-game show. The one year anniversary of the attacks on New York remained three days away. Police were everywhere, I thought. I thought about getting one to help us. To help the others, who I assumed were right behind me since the path from underground was so clear and bright. But my friends did not follow me up.

The police officers didn't notice that I'd just left the underground New York jazz club without paying for my Martini. Didn't notice that I didn't pay the cover charge or half the cover charge. Didn't notice that I'd sat above spilled toilet water in a New York jazz club and talked with a Wall Street manager of the Latin American Division, his model wife, a rhetorician, and a vascular surgeon—talked louder than the music. Didn't notice that I stood alive on 7th Avenue in the night before the opening football game with imperceptible stolen alcohol circulating in my uncharted arteries. They didn't notice me at all.

I noticed each of them: police poised to defend against both overt and invisible attacks. But they didn't see me. It's not that they couldn't, but they weren't looking for me. They hadn't heard that I talked loudly and drank freely and laughed openly and walked up from underground without paying for my one cool drink without a cover or half off the cover charge.

I walked past a police officer, a woman, and looked directly at her. She looked up 7th Avenue.

I saw my friends. They had initially followed me toward the door above until her husband looked back once and noticed his model wife talking to the manager. She felt an ethical obligation to pay for the drinks we'd ordered. That seemed fair, in her sole judgment. Seemed right. Since I had already disappeared, the vascular surgeon went back and paid for my drink. No one paid the cover. The manager agreed.

We met on the street. They told me what happened underground. How they almost made it out. Made it up. She, the wife, the model, the model wife, did right, Man, she stopped and talked to the manager and smiled and played him a song about the drinks and New York and jazz and didn't mention the toilet water and the new waitress when she smiled a professional smile that belonged on a billboard on Broadway or else a magazine ad.

The vascular surgeon went home to his wife in their upper East Side apartment the size of my Edison living room. She remained asleep, oblivious to the jazz scene.

Alejandro and his model wife went home, too.

I flew out of New York, back to Sacramento, after Serena beat Venus for the US Open tennis title. Aretha Franklin sang the national anthem before the New York final. We heard the fire works shoot into the sky as Franklin lifted the final note. It was important that the announcer, who introduced Aretha, Serena, and Venus, forewarned the audience that sudden, unexpected blasts were to be expected.

CONFESSIONS II

Edison Elementary School provided him with vision tests as a child. He saw things that others could not see until they were upon them. These others could neither verify with their own eyes, nor with the eyes of others, the existence of things whose clarity tormented him. They refused to believe he could see things that did not exist. Though she could not interpret his fantastic vision in utero, even his mother, a small woman, alone, except for the fetus in her womb, suspected he could see. During his elementary school years, before Edison referred him to an area optometrist, his teachers sat him in front of the class because they were convinced he could not see the board from any farther back. But in middle school, during a routine English course, his teacher reassigned him to the back of the class because she felt his stare penetrated beneath her outer layers. The importance of this move was not that he could not see her from the back of the room; but that she could not see him. In the eleventh grade, in the only episode of absurdity he acknowledged, a substitute teacher predicted he was blind because she could not see something he described as large as life. This convinced the substitute teacher that this "vision" could only have originated where it remained: in the mind of C. Reginald Globle.

Edison is a little town. I ran along the levee breathing heavily as I inhaled the aromatic chips from pastures lining the tributary leading to the Bay. Many years later, now, as I jog outside the elite neighborhood, I smell the same aroma rising from the pretty colored foliage along the periphery of the fertilized homes. I don't see C. Reginald Globle anymore. I last saw him during the eighth grade at Port of the Valley Middle School when I worked as a butcher at Star Market.

He pushed a previously silver rusted metal shopping cart from the store throughout the south side of Edison. The cart, usually half-filled with aluminum cans, clear glass bottles, and green glass bottles, appeared to belong to him. The cart was a remnant from the first year Star Market opened it's door on Edison's south side. It was the only one surviving from the days before the fire that burned all the old carts—all, except this one, which the owner never bothered him about returning. He reasoned that C. Reginald Globle saved it from the fire and let him keep it.

C. Reginald Globle brought the cans and bottles to the store everyday for redemption. He spent the redeemed money right there in Star Market at the butcher counter where he bought chicken backs for his small, alone mother to cook. The redeemed money never left the store.

Can I have thirty-eight cents' worth of chicken backs? His voice spoke just above a whisper. I didn't actually hear him the first time he ordered the chicken backs. So he spoke louder to me.

I had only been working at the butcher counter for a few days when he placed this order. The owner moved me there after I failed in every other department. I failed fruits the first day I got hired. What does a 14 year old know about stacking fruit in a nutritious pyramid so that the whims of gravity don't call them back to the floor? I failed shelving because I didn't present the good side of the round cans to the customers. I don't remember how I failed refrigeration. I think the owner blamed me when the milk went bad. I do remember being moved to the refrigerator from the canned section. I came to love the cold during the summer of my first job in hot Edison where the milk must have gone bad because he moved me to boxes next. I lifted them off the truck, stacked them, opened them, emptied them, flattened the empty boxes, and put them in a machine that smashed them together and tied them with a plastic band into a cardboard cube the same size as the emptied box began. I was no good at this. The owner tried me at the cash register because he noticed my unforetold ease with numbers. In the end, I was too accurate with the change. Though I never made a calculating mistake, he moved me to the meat counter—my last chance to work at a job I never wanted. I spoke to C. Reginald

Globle during my last hour as a cashier when he came to redeem his cans and bottles. He placed the white meat package with the charge written with a black grease pen on the counter. A can of beans. Maybe a loaf of bread. I rang him up. Collected the money I had just given him a few minutes earlier for his collected cans and bottles. I didn't know what was in the white meat package until the owner moved me to the meat section of the store. I wondered which meat could cost only thirty-six cents.

He ordered the chicken backs.

I reached past the chicken legs, thighs, breasts, wings, and necks into the meat and grabbed a few chicken backs from their pan. I didn't know how many would weigh 38 cents. Or 42 cents. Or, when the people were thirsty and left more bottles and cans on the sticky Edison road, a dollar's worth. This day it was a dollar's worth. So I grabbed as many chicken backs as I could fit in one fist. The points of the splintered chicken ribs poked into my fingers. Past the necks, the wings, the breasts, the thighs, and the legs, I brought the backs forward, out of the refrigerated meat case, and weighed them. The price was a penny over the one dollar he requested. I don't know if he saw that on the electric meat scale from his side of the counter but I quickly wrapped them and wrote "$1.00" on the white meat-wrapping paper with the black grease pen.

I looked at the world the way I had always looked at it: as if it didn't look back at me. C. Reginald Globle came to the meat counter and ordered one dollar's worth of chicken backs. I saw him. I heard him. I gave him the backs. And I asked him the most penetrating question I'd ever asked anyone in my entire 14 years: You ever think about buying a breast?

He smiled. Said nothing.

I saw him. Everywhere in south Edison. Walking with his shopping cart. Walking without it. Sometimes he saw me and smiled. Hello. Usually he didn't see me because he was looking at the ground trying to find an empty bottle. He preferred bottles because he could redeem them for more money than cans. But he accepted either. I saw him even when he didn't see me.

I saw C. Reginald Globle on a south side Sunday morning as I rounded the corner to open the meat case at Star Market. C. Reginald Globle stood still and watched a discarded man dressed in a forgotten green Army jacket. The man, wrapped in the filth of south Edison, intoxicated from the years before. Or else, from earlier that south Sunday morning in a renewed drunken state, the discarded man stood unaware of C. Reginald Globle's fantastic sight. The south Edison man stood for an eternal instant holding a green bottle turned up to his lips, his head tilted back as he poured the green bottle's drink into his throat. While pouring from above, the man liberated his member from the green fatigues and, without deliberation, excreted a steady arc of thick green urine.

I don't know whether he was waiting to see if the discarded man would leave the green bottle on the ground, or if C. Reginald Globle simply appreciated the fantastic stream from the fatigued man's free member.

I saw him in class every school day. He sat behind me each year since the first grade. But I only shared one of the six classes in the eighth grade. I don't remember him wearing glasses in elementary school, but by the time we were in junior high, he wore them. He asked the teacher for a piece of masking tape when the plastic frames broke. I began wearing glasses in the second grade. My vision declined each year until a surgeon returned it with an invisible knife. Now I see with impossible clarity.

Children teased his name in elementary school the way children do: Globle became Globble became Gobble became Gobble Gobble. The other children in grade school would run past him on the playground and speak like turkeys: Gobble Gobble. I don't think they saw him; but I can't be certain.

I didn't do this. My mind had always conflated his name with Global.

What's he going to do with all that money? I heard the owner say when C. Reginald Global redeemed the discarded bottles.

Buy some chicken backs, I said.

The Director of Meats received a call from a Chinese restaurant for a special order of chicken feet for a soup. About a week later I opened the case of chicken feet. I'd never considered a solitary chicken foot before this. I stood in awe of an entire case of chicken feet. I picked one up by what would have been the lower shin and brought it close to my eyes. I squeezed the tendons and watched the free claws grasp at nothing.

I released the tendons. And squeezed again. I imagined a chicken walking, each step clawing at the ground to move forward. I heard the owner coming and thought I'd get moved to sweeping the parking lot if he caught me playing with the chicken. So I grabbed a metal pan and filled it with the feet. I placed the pan of feet in the front of the meat case below the thighs and legs where potential customers could see them. I thought this was tactically onomatopoeic. This inadvertent foresight of mine worked in the end because the restaurant owner canceled the order. So we had to try to sell the chicken feet to the customers who lived in south Edison. But they didn't buy the feet. Only C. Reginald Global did. He thought he could get more soup for less money if he used the feet, which were cheaper than the backs. In the end, this didn't work. C. Reginald Global decided to spend more money and go back to the backs.

When no one was looking, I wrapped a filet mignon in the white meat-wrapping paper and wrote "38 CENTS" on it with a black grease pen. I placed the filet in the lower part of the meat case so that I could pay for it at the end of the day and take it home. I'd not yet tasted filet by then, but didn't want to pay what the Director of Meats considered a just amount.

I didn't see him standing in front of the meat case. When I stood up straight after kneeling to put the cheapened filet in the lower case, he was there. I don't know if he saw me. C. Reginald Global whispered an order for a few cents' worth of chicken backs. I didn't look at him. I grabbed a handful and could not feel the chicken ribs poking into my hand.

I gave him the package and washed what I thought was chicken blood off of my hands.

It was my blood.

Although the cheapened filet was behind the metal door of the refrigerated meat case, I saw it everywhere. The Director of Meats found the wrapped filet marked "38 CENTS" and asked me if I knew who put it there. I confessed it was mine.

Without opening the filet, he said, I'm glad you decided to take some of these chicken feet home. No one else wants them.

I didn't know if C. Reginald Global would tell the owner what he saw. I didn't think he would. And I wasn't even sure he saw anything. He might have been blind to the cheapened filet. Blind to me.

Poor poor without hope but without bitterness because there was no hope with green bottles and a man urinated on my side of town enough money to pay for a little chicken meat attached to chicken ribs with the black grease pen I wrote invisible numbers and no one saw my thirtyeightcents on the white meat black grease the owner wouldnt see me and charge me more more filet chicken mignon worth aluminum bottles and green cans and cheap chicken feet and cheap chicken backs for south Edison stew yes I saw him and he saw me and I waited until no one saw me unwrap the meat eat meat and put it back so someone could pay just money full price yes.

C. Reginald Global went to the meat counter and ordered a dollar's worth of chicken backs. I reached into the meat case and grabbed two breasts. I wrapped them in meat-wrapping paper and wrote "$1.00" without weighing the breasts. He didn't see me not weigh the breasts.

He wouldn't see them until he got home and unwrapped the package. I quit my job that night when I was 14. I didn't see him at school again. I don't know what happened to C. Reginald Global. I decided he should eat breasts for dinner.

THE AUTOBIOGRAPHY OF
MARK WHITE AS TOLD
TO RICHARD GARCIA

I wanted him to write the book, but he refused. I pressed that his story was valuable, important, exciting. That people would want to read it. But he persisted in full disagreement: "I'm a university professor. There's nothing exciting about my life."

As I recounted his stories that he'd told me through the years since we met at Berkeley, he found my versions of his stories interesting, even funny, at times. But I could not persuade him to write the book. I didn't think of it as a memoir of a famous person, or an autobiography of someone who'd lived in extreme conditions—say, a slave narrative like Frederick Douglas'. Or even as a self-portrait by Van Gogh. Neither did I imagine a chronicle of a good man's events that start in the beginning and lead to the end.

But, an autobiography, nevertheless.

The arguments I attempted with this professor of argument necessarily missed my mark. That is, Mark White, professor of rhetoric, thinks of communication in classical rhetorical terms: speaker, speech, audience. If I was the speaker and he was the audience, then the speech—my argument that he should write his own autobiography—remained inadequate. His analysis of my speech always prevailed over my ambition to read his story.

I argued that his life would be interesting to freshman English students in Los Angeles. Or else, graduate students in Durham. An intense writing program at a small New England college. He could even teach his own text at his university. Some teenager would receive his words about words and be inspired to consider self-education instead of the alternative.

"I'm a professor without tenure. I teach students about argument. I have debt. Haven't lived an especially exciting life. Why would anyone want to read my story? More to the point: Why would I want to write it?"

Our conversations went this way for more than three years. In fact, I brought it up less and less as we talked about tenure, publications, promotions, salary, progress. Even the content of our conversations remained limited to real estate, economics, America, race, Ellison, and the world. In one desperate phone call, we found ourselves citing Douglas' narrative about being free: "It's a shame that we're using a slave narrative to illustrate our condition as minority faculty. And we're identifying with it!"

We laughed and snatched ourselves back into the present. No slaves here. But these past words seemed intended for a present audience who might understand their application.

■ ■ ■

Mark White is nearly finished with his academic work: a big book on Malcolm X. This book was to be the definitive rhetorical work on Malcolm. I tried, again, to convince him that he should write his own autobiography when he finished Malcolm. But when he looked at the life of someone like Malcolm X, Mark White considered that his own life story would not be worthy by comparison.

That's when I got the title for my book. Playfully, I told him that I'd write the big book and call it *The Autobiography of Mark White as told to Richard Garcia.* As an authority on Malcolm, he instantly recognized the reference. This held his attention. But Mark White worried that I, like him, would not have much to say about his life.

I remembered some stories he'd told me beginning with ones I heard while we were both still at Berkeley. Once I had his permission to write the book, I felt a facility to remember. However, soon after I began writing, I realized I could not remember them in the order they happened. Neither could I remember them in the order he told them to me. Rather, I remembered them at all once. This would challenge the timing of events in the book. An anachronistic autobiography, then. I thought I could write it first as memory allowed the events to be typed. I'd then rearrange the chapters so that the book would make chronologic sense. Mark White remained pessimistic that such a book could ever be successful. I wanted to get some things cleared up in a sort of interview before I started writing. However, I never could get him to provide the details of his disfellowship from the church. When I asked why the Jehovah's Witnesses expelled him, he recalled a story from graduate school when his old professor taught Milton's sonnet, "On Time." I don't remember the precise discourse that preceded his professor's declaration, but the class had been discussing the sonnet with some clarity when the professor illustrated the sonnet's end. Mark White's professor read the part of the sonnet and spoke of Milton's use of chance and time:

Then all this Earthy grosnes quit,
Attir'd with Stars, we shall for ever sit,
Triumphing over Death, and Chance, and thee O Time.

For nearly thirty years, including in this class, the old professor taught that no one knew what Milton's "chance" referenced. Mark White interrupted the old professor's narrative to disagree: "He's talking about Ecclesiastes here. Surely Milton's intended audience would have understood the reference, even if our modern university professor does not. Does anyone have a Bible?" (This was not an unusual question to ask in a graduate seminar in the Berkeley Rhetoric

Department. One of the other four graduate students, the woman, produced a Bible she carried around with her.) Mark White turned to Ecclesiastes and found Milton's "chance" reference. "Yes, here it is."

Ecclesiastes 9:11
I returned, and saw under the sun, that the race
is not to the swift, nor the battle to the strong,
neither yet bread to the wise, nor yet riches to men of
understanding, nor yet favour to men of skill; but time
and chance happeneth to them all.

Naturally, the old professor was both impressed and disturbed. Within days he submitted the new analysis for publication without giving Mark White credit. This sort of procedure seemed understandable and routine within the academy as far as Mark White could tell at the time.

"But how did you know this was Milton's reference if you hadn't read the sonnet before that afternoon?"

"I didn't say I *understood* the reference; I only recognized from whence he took it. When I was a child, I read the Bible in church. I read it twice by the time I dropped out of high school. I know all the books. I'd even read it while I was supposed to be listening to the minister. Actually, I read the Old Testament for the sex and violence; but who's going to disturb a child reading the Bible in church? My parents just left me alone."

This, of course, became valuable to me when, many years later, I asked Mark White to explain why Morrison used the name Shadrach in her second novel. Mark White seemed surprised that I didn't know the story of King Nebuchadnezzar. "Don't you remember? He sent the three of them, Shadrach, Meshach, and Abednego, into the furnace because they would not worship him. But God went along and didn't let them burn. King Nebuchadnezzar saw four in the furnace."

"I was raised Catholic. What do I know about the Old Testament? Anyway, I left Catholicism probably about the same time you were disfellowshiped. Why was that, again?"

Fortuitously, his explanation of the furnace unraveled a narrative plot difficulty I was having with my own novel at the time. In my version of the furnace, three Mexican men went in. Without knowing anything at all about King Nebuchadnezzar and the four he saw in the furnace, my version had only the three Mexicans, and no God. I thought that in order to be consistent with the reference, which I didn't know at the time I wrote that scene, I should include a fourth Mexican in a revision. But, as I considered my narrative with Mark White's lesson about the Old Testament in mind, I chose to let the three Mexicans enter the oven alone. However, like Shadrach, Meshach, and Abednego, my Mexicans didn't burn.

■　■　■

Mark White's knowledge is wide and deep, without ceremony. He read the Bible in church because he didn't want to be there. I never thought of this as a perversion; rather, I admired his private education. Without acknowledging it at the time, Mark White, too, believed that all education is private. No teacher, no parent, no sister, no classmate, no friend, no professor ever knew the breadth of his knowledge. I urged him to write for popular journals or newspapers as a retort to some of the commentaries that threaten decency and intelligence, not to mention sheer insight. Of course, he declined. Not because he didn't have anything to say in disagreement; not because he couldn't say things with more clarity and persuasion; and not because he wasn't concerned about decency or insight; but because he was not interested in writing on the present as a topic.

He left high school with a 0.7 GPA. While he didn't read the assigned readings, he made himself expert in Aristotelian poetics, King Lear, and Wordsworth, among the others. I thought all of this would make his autobiography interesting, saleable. During the summer after he dropped out of high school, Mark White trained as a welder. That same year the University of California offered two scholarships to Bay Area applicants who scored highest on a test they gave. I believe this was the only year this sort of test was offered, and don't recall the reason it was pulled from circulation. In any case, Mark White's mother, who knew her son to be clever, and thought he could pass any test he found interesting, read about the offer at the Post Office where she worked. Mark White scored the highest in the region, just above his Mexican friend. They both went to

Berkeley the next fall. But because Mark White didn't understand the inner workings of a university, he simply enrolled in classes that appeared interesting to him as he flipped through the Schedule of Classes. Afro-American Literature, Rhetoric, Wordsworth, and one other class. He got an A in each of these first four classes founded in pure ignorance. By the end of his sophomore year someone pointed out some university logistics and urged him to take the breadth requirements. By his senior year, a professor in the Rhetoric Department informed him of the letter of recommendation he'd written on Mark White's behalf. "I wrote the letter, but the Rhetoric Department hasn't received your application to graduate school yet. You'd better get on it. I believe the deadline has already passed." Mark White never considered graduate school until that hallway discourse. He was still in the process of applying when he received his anachronistic letter of acceptance.

▪ ▪ ▪

I included these, and other, events in the big book I wrote. While it received some critical recognition upon its publication, *The Autobiography of Mark White as told to Richard Garcia*, never enjoyed popular success. Now out of print, it remains in some university libraries, and a few bookstores. I heard of one course in Upper Massachusetts that offered it as suggested reading, but no list of required texts. In the end, it appears, Mark

White was correct. Only a handful of academics are interested in this autobiography.

After his successful tenure review he concentrated on his Malcolm X book, which was in progress at the time of the review. He wanted the book to build such that, for example, when the reader gets to Chapter 9, she'd appreciate having read chapter 8 because 9 depends on everything before it. He wanted to publish the definitive academic book on Malcolm X's rhetoric.

I argued the same for the book about Mark White, but he declined: "I'm talking about a mountain verses a hill, he said. Certainly Malcolm X is a mountain."

"But I think Mark White is a mountain."

"There's Mount Everest, and then there's Mount Diablo."

The movement of his chapters build upon each preceding chapter rather than a disjointed collection. They show evolution. One part depends on what came before, and is necessary for what comes next. Not just a collection.

This Malcolm book is only a part of his real ambition: a book on African American Communication where the Malcolm X book would be a small part—say, Chapter 15, or so—of this bigger book. Then, a definitive book that begins in Africa with oral narratives, song, folk stories, poetry, music, sermon, spiritual, et cetera. A much bigger book. Comprehensive again. A whole book, not a collection or part. African American Communication—from African past to American present. Story as continuum. "I'll create the standard in the field. The Malcolm book will be a brief part of this exhaustive book."

Talking about this future book depressed him. He had not made the progress he'd hoped even on the Malcolm book, so could not earnestly consider the second.

■ ■ ■

Mortality is the issue here. Time is the variable. And chance.

Mark White's illness progressed as he wrote his book on Malcolm's rhetoric. He doesn't think he'll get to African American Communication, the exhaustive book that doesn't exist, before he dies. I picked up my copy of *The Autobiography of Mark White as told to Richard Garcia* and looked at the back cover. I thought about the privileged personal anecdotes I disclosed inside. I had not read the book in several years. I didn't see the point. I know him. I wrote the book. I knew the stories even better than they were typed in the pages of the book. I decided to read my book again. Maybe I could restructure it, update it, make it better. A second edition, then. I wanted to see where I might be able to add, delete, correct, or improve the old prose. A re-timing. Like an old jazz piece re-timed for a present audience who might not appreciate the original. I began flipping through the pages in a cursory, yet curious, way. I skimmed over some of the sentences. They seemed fine as they were. I could not see where

I might change anything as an editor of a second or third edition of a big text might. So, I went back to the beginning of Chapter 1 and read the anachronistic autobiography chronologically to the end. I found that one chapter was necessary for the next. But I re-timed the book anyway. I rearranged the chapters, clarified the details of his disfellowship, made some sentences more precise, made some less, and changed the ending, entirely. This book was decisively different from the original version of *The Autobiography of Mark White as told to Richard Garcia.* However, when I compared it with the original text, I could not decipher any changes at all in the second edition.

ONE GREEN EYE

A thin man is sitting three chairs away from me at the bar, waiting for the jazz singer's climb up to the stage. The man has a skinny face with a lined beard. He's smoking a cigarette with a long ash, suspended, bending toward the ground. The ash passively falls. I don't remember him flicking it.

The waiter brings me a glass of Chardonnay. But I'd ordered red wine. I point to the drink written in the menu. He gives me the other glass of red wine from his tray. I ask him what it is because I don't just want any red wine that he happens to have on his tray, but the one I ordered. "It's that gentleman's drink. He ordered the same red wine. I'm sorry for my confusion. I'll give you his and get him another." I look again at the man. The waiter gives him his demitasse of espresso, says something, and goes to get the red wine like mine.

The man at the bar looks like a burned out musician. I can't tell if he's done heroin before. He's not my father. Anyway, my father couldn't grow a beard. My mother told me that he had one green eye and one brown eye. He's dead now.

My daughter was born with blue eyes. Then, within two or three months they changed to gray. Now her eyes are both green. My eyes are both brown. The red wine is almost gone. The man's cigarette ash passively falls. The lights go down. My father is dead. The jazz singer is climbing to the stage.

Jazz Women Trio

Meshell Ndegeocello held her electric bass silent with possibility. With both hands at the back of the stage in the dark room she stood wearing an orange beanie cap with what appeared to be a blue ball on top. I could see her easily from my seat, elevated but close to the stage. She closed her eyes, prepared her left finger tips along the length of the electric bass strings and held her right ones, firm and flaccid, at once, poised to create the sound that would stop the silence originating only an instant before, when the people finished applauding as she walked onto the stage.

I'd made reservations on the Blue Note website while still in Edison the month before. But when we arrived at the New York door, the doorman informed us: Meshell won't be singing tonight.

I asked if we could get our money back since I purchased them online three thousand miles ago fully expecting to see Ms. Ndegeocello in person. Amidst my confusion, the doorman clarified that Meshell would indeed be there that night, but would be playing electric bass, not vocals. Both his physical and verbal stances indicated that he'd already heard this from the people ahead of me; and that he'd be willing to refund my money should I ask.

Since I think of myself as a real jazz fan, I agreed to stay for the show. Of course I'd enjoy hearing her play bass. The truth is I didn't know she played any instrument at all. I thought she was a singer. Jazz, soul, whatever she chose. I thought she played voice only. I own five of her CDs and didn't know this about her. I didn't let on. I thanked the doorman, gave him our tickets, and listened as he directed us to our seats.

A couple sat at our table. A small table with four chairs—two on each side facing each other—backed up to other chairs with no room to walk. The best part is that this table, while in the second section, was elevated above the first section, and near the side of the stage where Meshell Ndegeocello was to stand with her bass in silence before she rubbed the still strings.

The woman was decidedly darker than her boyfriend, who appeared too in love. As we approached, the young dark woman sat upright and sweetly asked our permission allowing them to sit next to each other on the same side of the table, as the seating was structured for couples to sit across from each other. Of course, we let them sit there, with their backs to the silent stage; and we sat next to each other facing the stage.

The four of us chatted as the crowd grew slowly. The waitress took our dinner and drink orders.

Where are you from? Where are you from? Have you seen her before? No, have you? I have five of her CDs, but I didn't know she played the bass. What do you do? What do you do? What do you do? What do you do? How long have you lived in New York? How long are you visiting here? Is this your first time? No. I like plays. I've seen RENT six times. I should see it. I should see something else. I've never been to the Village Vanguard. There are other Blue Notes around the world. Have you seen Joshua Redman?

The young woman, an interpreter, said she is from Colombia. As I do with any Colombian, I informed her that I am a great Gabriel Garcia Marquez fan. We named our son Gabriel!

My wife looked at me with leniency.

The Colombian young woman interpreter told us that she'd met Gabriel Garcia Marquez once, while translating for the government. I forgot where they were. But he was talking and she went up to him with the excitement of returning home from a long trip.

I was blown away. I walked up and told him that I'm from Cartagena. He looked at me and said, How come I don't know you? Who's your family?

She told him of her parents, aunts, uncles, cousins, street, house, school, play, friends until he recognized her entire lineage even better than she did and finished her story for her.

I listened to the Colombian interpreter tell me the fantastic tale of a meeting I could never imagine.

As I listened to sounds of Marquez while I awaited Ndgeocello's entrance into the warm room filling with people and stories about the edges of Colombia and California. I wondered if what the doorman said was true: Meshell will sing at least one song, so don't worry.

Since I memorized all her songs I'd heard, I hoped to see her sing them close to their existence inside my memory. Of course, in a live performance, the notes are nuanced and bent slightly to remind us we are alive. These are the parts I remember most when listening to a singer, say Sarah Vaughan, sing a live version of a recorded song. Since I've never seen Ms. Vaughan in person, I try to compare her various live recordings of Once in a While. I nearly saw her at what was to be her final concert during my senior year at the University. I was just beginning to become a jazz fan and, as I recall, just ending a semester, and perfectly poor. So, I did not attend the concert. I did not understand what I'd missed when she died. But as time for me continues I listen and miss her voice. The more I listen to her recorded voice, the more I regret missing her in life.

This night, I'd hoped, would be different. I imagined that Ms. Ndegeocello would play many songs on the bass and delight us in the end with a vocal or two. As I listened to the voice of the woman from Cartagena, I secretly waited to hear the singer's live voice. But the more she talked about Marquez talking about her family, the less I thought about the singer's voice.

We'd finished our first drinks. We were finishing our dinner. The waitress took our second drink orders. As she brought them, just before the collective was to enter the room, I no longer waited to hear the singer's voice. I watched her enter the dark room and decided the music would be enough.

Meshell Ndegeocello and her band walked out together. Since she was the star, I imagined she'd allow them to walk out first, then follow in a special walk. But I recognized the integrated collective move from a previous show with Joshua Redman and his group. She came out wearing an orange beanie cap and a zipped-up sweat suit, made her way to the back of the stage, picked up her bass, looked into the crowd, and closed her eyes in silence.

VALLEY FEVER

"Pestilence" is strictly a biblical word. "No pestilence shall fall on the land." This is an example of the way the word is used in a sentence. But a church sentence, not a real one. Not a sentence where two people are talking with each other; but one where the speaker is speaking—whether the audience is listening, understanding, or speaking back is negligible. It's a word that warns of plague on a people without consideration of the individual in particular. In fact, on the land is not where the insult is threatened, but on people. "No pestilence on the land," then, is a position statement meant to protect people, not soil. Who among us can protect against pestilence? God, then. It's God talking. Whether people believe in God does not concern the speaker in the least.

Coccidiomycosis is not really a pest. It's more of a fungus. In the soil, where it lives naturally. In the hot San Joaquin Valley of central California: Home of Cocci. More a part of the everyday soil than an organism that descends upon a land. It's already here. Has always been here. As much a part of the earth as the earth itself. One with the people. Most of us who are born here developed anything from a mild respiratory infection as children—not even suspected to be *coccidiomycosis* by the local general doctor—to a full-blown pulmonary infection resulting in death—clearly diagnosed, yet impervious to the cadre of doctors who didn't specialize in anything at all. Death from Valley Fever. But that's rare. Most get what is commonly called a cold by the local cadre of doctors who didn't specialize in anything at all. A cold that can't be helped. This is acceptable to the people here because, like a cold, nothing can be done about Cocci either. Nothing, that is, unless the person begins to die. Then there are a number of schemes the doctors connive. None to save the people. Either way, if cocci doesn't kill the person—which, as I said, is rare—antibodies form against it.

This is typical: antibodies against cocci form with even the slightest exposure. The antibodies form from memory cells and protect the person against future infections, like a vaccine: forever. Even better than a vaccine, which is not forever. Then, a simple "cold," that was really cocci, leaves a person in the California Central Valley immune to Valley Fever forever. Everyone who was born here is naturally exposed to Valley Fever, and all have antibodies to cocci.

Except me.

I was born normally. Played in the dirt with all the other kids. Got as many colds and pulmonary infections as anyone on the south side of Edison. In fact, I suffered from an undiagnosed chronic allergic condition since I was about six years old. A cadre of doctors who did not specialize in anything at all ran tests on me and my blood to find which allergens might have caused my recurrent respiratory infections. They found nothing. Finally, while interned at the Valley Pulmonary Ward for seven days, the Chief of Medicine ordered a blood test to definitively establish cocci as the cause of all my troubles. The laboratory returned the results of my blood test within three days: Negative. I had no antibodies to *coccidiomycosis*. The results meant that I had never been exposed to cocci. But this could not be true since I was born here. There must be a lab error, the Chief of Medicine thought. He reordered the blood test.

Still Negative.

By this time he'd given up on diagnosing the precise cause of this particular pulmonary infection. He consulted with an immunologist from the big city to help him figure out why I had no antibodies to cocci.

I don't remember how long I stayed interned on the Pulmonary Ward while he and the immunologist from the city ran their tests, but the Unit Secretary finally informed the doctors that I was entirely well, and should be sent home from the hospital. The Chief found no evidence in my medical record to refute her, so he discharged me at once.

I went back to school the next day. I believe I'd already started eighth grade by this discharge. I read what I could find on Valley Fever, which wasn't much. I found a sentence that disturbed me: Filipinos succumbed to Valley Fever more than any other group. I'd never considered Filipinos a group, however, since we all invisibly grew up together. I asked my Filipino friend what he knew about this plague on Filipinos. He knew nothing.

The temperature gets high in the valley. Summer heat rises from the asphalt in waves visible to my naked eye if I crouch down and look at the earth horizontally. The distorted clarity of people and things beyond the heat is blurred by the fever rising from the valley floor. All get immunity against Cocci, except the ones who die. I don't know why some get a more serious infection than others. Neither do I know why Filipinos are especially endangered. The Public Health Officer is looking into this. He has other things to look into, however, so gets back to this question each time there is an outbreak at Valley Hospital. More than a few cases, and he's on it again. Always, however, with the same results. Mexicans are least affected by Valley Fever. The field workers are even less affected. The more contact with Cocci, the better. Memory cells and antibodies protect them. Except me. The immunologist ran tests of my antibodies against other organisms that time I was interned on the Pulmonary Ward and found that I'm immune to everything else in his battery. But not Cocci. He reported the absence of my antibodies to both the state and federal Offices of Outbreak Control, and asked if either had heard of this before. No one bothered to reply.

The Chief of Medicine diagnosed another case of Valley Fever. A Filipino teenager who, as an infant, moved to the valley with his parents from San Jose, where he was born. Before that, his parents moved to San Jose from a small town outside of Manila. I don't remember the name. I remember he told me that his father played basketball on his street with slippers. He moved to San Jose with his wife, who delivered their son, Christopher Columbus Ramirez, within a couple of years. Chris' parents moved to the San Joaquin Valley to pick asparagus. They told him to become a doctor so that he wouldn't have to pick asparagus when he grew up. He believed them, studied, took only college prep courses, and declined to attend the asparagus festival each spring. I had no desire to become a doctor, but took the same classes as Chris because we were both good at math. Because of Chris, I took two years of math in the tenth grade so that we could take calculus as seniors. I didn't know what calculus was. But Chris warned that without calculus, he'd end up picking asparagus. This meant nothing to me. Like my family before me, I expected to remain in the valley forever. I took the two years of math anyway. So, strictly because Chris didn't want to pick asparagus, by the time I was a senior, I was prepared to attend any university in America. Maybe anywhere on English-speaking earth. (I didn't check.) And if he hadn't died of Valley Fever, I believe Chris would have become a doctor. However, without confessing to his parents, he secretly considered a career in computers.

Chris' wasn't the only death by Cocci that year. The Chief discovered another person with unexplained fever. His tests confirmed Cocci. An older woman, also Filipino, unrelated to Chris, died the next week. The Chief contacted the immunologist when the third person with a cough and an unexplained fever was referred to his Pulmonary clinic. He admitted this man, a Mexican from the pomodoro tomato fields, to the Intensive Care Unit and called both the immunologist and the local Public Health Officer. The three of them drafted reports, called centers scattered around the country, consulted other experts in both Immunology and Infectious Diseases. Nothing. No one could save the Mexican man. More presented and died: Black, White, Mexican, Filipino, and one older Japanese woman. The Valley Times reported the growing number and provided the readers with information about Valley Fever; urged them to see their doctors early if they suspected they might have Valley Fever, even if the doctors would be unable to help. By Monday morning all the lines to doctors' offices were busy with people who had seasonal allergies, sore throats, tuberculosis, undiagnosed asthma, and nothing wrong at all. This last group was the most difficult to treat: they had no disease, but would not get off of the phone because they wanted the doctors to explain all that was known, and all that was not known, about Valley Fever, so they could watch for the invisible plague. People with actual Valley Fever could not reach their doctors because all the lines were tied up. So, they drove themselves or their children to the hospitals and waited in rooms filled with people who could not reach their doctors by phone.

The local news stations ran a piece about the plague on Friday night. A Brokowesque newscaster interviewed a clinical professor of Infectious Diseases, some patients with masks, the immunologist, one resident in training who spoke more of the exciting learning cases that would make him a better doctor in the future than about this particular disease in the present, and the Chief of Medicine.

Years passed. Textbooks were amended because of this peculiar expression of Valley Fever that was previously unknown. The San Joaquin Valley became known outside of California. And, even within California, people began to recognize the Valley for more than its proximity to Lake Tahoe skiing, Yosemite hiking, San Francisco eating.

I've been through there on my way to somewhere else.

Cool Hand Luke was filmed there, right?

Wasn't there a boxer from the valley?

Didn't Richard Rodriguez grow up out there?

I heard a jazz trumpeter there once.

The Chief of Medicine studied my blood. Sent it to the university lab. Sent it to the scattered centers. Referred me to regional immunologists to establish an explanation for why I get every other infection that passes through the valley; I suffer from chronic allergies that have left me with a crippling nasal drip;

I cough and wheeze at the slightest provocation by our imperceptible pollen or the Delta breeze; I itch; I limp; and my large intestine cramps in a violent twist with either milk or broccoli.

But my antibody titers to Cocci remain zero. I have no memory cells.

No one has died from Valley Fever since the plague that killed Chris. Some still get fever. Some live with a subclinical cough. People seem to have forgotten about Cocci. When my uncle died the cadre of doctors who didn't specialize in anything at all decided it was his heart, and not his lungs. He drank; so maybe that had something to do with it. I don't remember if he'd had a fever. I don't remember the particulars of time when I was interned on the Pulmonary Ward while the Chief and the immunologist from the city ran their tests before the Unit Secretary finally informed the doctors that my fever was gone and that I should be sent home from the hospital. The Chief found no evidence in my medical record to refute her, so he discharged me to home. My fever was gone. Specialists study my diet, race, exercise, height, weight, alcohol use, birth weight, formula I drank as an infant. They ask if I smoke cigarettes, use street drugs. They ask about my family's medical history. I told them that my mother broke her ankle once. I have no bad habits that can account for my missing antibodies against Valley Fever.

SASSY

My father played a series of six CDs when I was two. He doesn't recall the singers, the songs, or the order. He only knows the six CDs were all jazz. He didn't play the music for my particular benefit, but to passively have music in our house, I suspect, for his benefit. About two weeks later, as he tells it, he noticed me singing: *Nice work if you can get it. And you can get it if you can.* He noticed that I even attempted—in my two year old voice—Billie Holiday's inflections.

Billie Holiday was there, in the beginning, I believe. Miles and the others, too. The musicians whirred as I got older. I don't think it's because the CD player was on random selection; rather, because jazz exists in my memory all at once.

My father worked on a screenplay about Sarah Vaughan. Though he was not a screenwriter, he contended—to me, my mother, anyone who would listen, and even some who would not listen—that Sarah Vaughan's story would make a great movie. Not because her timing, more than the others, invited the audience in. Not because her timbre deepened with time and cigarettes to a more intricate nearness. Not even because her life was an onomatopoeic version of America. I'm not sure how far he's gotten with that screenplay. I don't know if he'll ever finish, which is not really the attraction of screenplays. I do think he's right about Sassy. I've listened to him talk about her from the beginning of memory and I cannot distinguish her body from memories of real events. That is, stories about the chance he had to see her, segments of dialogue, American history, and her recorded voice are all one for me.

My mother took me to church, where my father didn't want to go. I joined the choir because my parents thought I'd be a good gospel singer. I did my best, which wasn't bad. Though I never told them, I confess I didn't feel like a gospel singer. I'd sneak jazz into the unnoticeable parts of songs so that the audience might accept my grace notes. I later sang in my high school jazz band. Some people noticed my voice was derivative of Sarah Vaughan's. They didn't not mean "derivative" with its negative connotation the way a writer who is considered derivative of, say, Borges, lacks both talent and an understanding of Schopenhauer. No. Being derivative of Sassy was a good thing, I thought.

But I didn't try to sing like Sarah Vaughan. I don't believe I sound like her at all. I imagine that listening to her recorded voice influenced my style the way

Faulkner influenced the past. So, the audience could at least be certain I am Sarah's fan.

All right.

What they don't hear is that my father's voice is the one I can't get out of my music. What tragedy foretells a man's life's work that goes unheard? Billie's moans, Sarah's depths, Miles' silent ways exist in him as he listens to me practice a brief solo or helps me interpret American History. Since I'd heard his interpretations so many times before, I paid more attention to the pauses in his narration, as they revealed my father to me more clearly. He's silent that way.

He's in the audience with my mother tonight. They travel to see most of my shows. It's nice for all of us when I play near home. I know he thinks of that time in college when he began to take on jazz. Sarah Vaughan was scheduled to play at the Greek Theater. He'd concentrated on the instrumentalists until then. I believe he didn't have much money toward the end of college, so decided to concentrate on her recordings and see her live the next time she was to play the Greek. He began to notice the personality of her voice that was independent of the lyrics or the music. Sarah Vaughan died before my father could ever hear her sing live. I see my parents sitting in the middle of the orchestra section as I step to the front of the stage.

Letter to Brodsky

*Ultimately, there should be a language
in which the word "egg" is reduced to O
entirely.*

— *Joseph Brodsky, 1996*
"Ab Ovo"

Joseph Brodsky died around the time my letter would
have arrived. That's what I thought when I read the
Valley Times. It's not that I think *words*, themselves,
could kill. That would be insane. Words are for the
living. No. I'm referring to the letter to Brodsky I sent
just before he died. The timing was a coincidence, I'm
sure. I'll say here, at the outset, I had not yet heard the
name Brodsky before I read his essay on identity. He
did not exist for me before then. Nor did his poetry. We
are not contemporaries. And I, for him, did not exist.

I was surrounded by the semester's books in my
room. I had been involved in what was to become my

decay from reading for several consecutive days when I discovered an essay about espionage written by Joseph Brodsky, a poet. I read his "Collector's Item" and knew from the opening line that I was instantly involved in an adventure in language I could not yet imagine. At first I couldn't tell why this essay differed from the rest. Content? Yes. But there was more. Within a few lines, it occurred to me that the *words* themselves—not their style, not their meanings, but the words—conjured me.

Before I could finish the essay, I turned to the back of the book to find the biographical notes on Joseph Brodsky: An exile from the Soviet Union. Teaches at Mount Holyoke College. Written books of poetry and essays. Won the Nobel Prize in Literature. How could this have gotten past me? If I was ever going to be a litterateur, at the very least, I should know the essentials.

So I read.

When I finished "Collector's Item," one thing was certain: I did not understand it. Brodsky used words which were, at once, foreign and familiar. Elusive yet precise. But I'm getting ahead of myself.

I deduced I was reading more than his words. "Collector's Item" is a story about a stamp and espionage and identity. Kim Philby's identity? Or Brodsky's? Or mine?

I should add here, since I'm referring to the prose of the poet: I have never understood a single stanza of poetry.

I decided to write to him. I'll write a letter to Brodsky. Yes. I'll ask for advice. For a suggestion. For a word.

I looked back to find the Russian. I made some calls and inevitably found the department secretary. And as she was being so helpful, I asked: "Professor Brodsky wouldn't be available to talk now, would he?" He was away on sabbatical. He was due back in winter to teach the spring semester. She assured me he would receive my letter:

January 11, 1996
Dear Professor Brodsky,

I am an exile like you. I'm in a labyrinth traveling freely between past and present without an ultimate destination.

I read Marquez, which naturally, led to Borges. Then Paz' essays, not his poetry, urged me deeper into my labyrinth. During the instant of eternity at the library I discovered an interview with Garcia Marquez which had been translated into English. He spoke of his predecessors: Woolf, Faulkner, Camus, and the others. I noticed Juan Rulfo, more than the others because he, above all, deals in the netherworld. So I read Rulfo. I then headed into the very mouth of my antiquity: Cervantes. I tussled with the ingenious layman and found that my labyrinth wasn't headed toward the Spain of antiquity at all.

Now I come to you, the Easterner. You wrote poetry in Cyrillic. Nothing could be farther from my reality. Ironically, it was this Cyrillic poetry that brought us together. Because of it, you were thrown out of Russia and ended up in the U.S. writing in English with the Latin alphabet. I don't mean to sound like a lunatic here. I found you entirely by accident. Your essay seemed a kind of infinity. As a young boy, I learned from the mathematicians that infinity is a space that can never be reached. As a young man, I learned from the poets that infinity is where we are. With your stories, I notice a face. I can't make it out entirely, though I suspect it's mine. I don't mean to impose,

I sent the letter to Brodsky. I didn't expect much. I gave up on that kind of thing a long time ago. I only hoped he would receive it. Maybe read it. Would he respond? Would he invite me to study with him and encourage me to chat with writers of antiquity? I sent the letter Mount Holyoke College.

His death occurred about this time. My letter should have arrived just as the professor returned from his absence. That's the time Joseph Brodsky suffered a massive heart attack and died.

I imagine you in your office at Mount Holyoke College reading through your mail that had piled up since you were last there. You arrive at my letter late in the afternoon of the day you die. You look at the return address and know instantly that it is a sad request from a would-be poet who wants to lean on your past for his present. This much I can understand. You open the letter and skim it. When you get to the labyrinthine part ending with you, you feel a kind of vague pressure in your chest that reminds you of the past. Given your heart condition, you know the past is here again. Always here.

Or else it happened another way. Could my letter still have been in the campus mailroom when you returned from where you were? Could it be that you never read my letter? Could you have died before you knew I existed? Certainly.

I discovered your Letter to Horace. Dead Horace of antiquity in the present. You didn't exist for Horace. You wrote in Latin, Horace. This brings us closer than I imagined. That is, at a certain point in the past, Spanish, of Latin extraction, was superimposed upon my antiquity. And so, in the end, Aztecs are related to ancient Rome. English is my language, my only hope of ever communicating with anyone in the past. At any rate, English is also the language Joseph chose when he wrote the letter to you. So, it doesn't seem to be a big leap to suggest that it is this English that brings us together, Horace.

I don't know if you read my letter before you died, Ioseph Brodsky. Although, I imagine you can read it now. I'm working on one to Cervantes. And Borges. Maybe Rulfo. I'll ask Paz if the other voice exists?

I read your poem today. "Ab Ovo." And then your "Lullaby."

Race

I

The test was brief. Only sixty seconds. The teacher who ran the Math Lab, as he called it, was not officially a math teacher. I can neither recall his title nor his agreement with the officials of the Edison Unified School District. I don't even believe he was official at all. This unofficial man gave us the math test. Twenty questions in sixty seconds, all answered correctly, wins a button. One wrong: no button. Twenty one seconds: no button. I started with the addition test. The unofficial man who ran the Math Lab gave me the Addition button. Then Subtraction. A button. Multiplication. Button. Division. Button. Near the end of the third grade I'd won all the buttons he had ending in Exponents, I believe. He created more tests for me and one other student, another third grader, who'd also earned all the buttons. He pushed us as far as we could go. Or else, as far as he could go. The final test: a word problem. This time only one. I noticed that this final question of the final test was an incorrect question. I don't see the need to explain the details here because I don't want anyone to mistake the point of this paragraph. Let me simply say that the question was a logical impossibility. Though he tried, the other third grader could make no sense of it, and offered an answer he knew was wrong. To explain something unexplainable here would bother me, the narrator, far more than it would bother you, the reader. So, the answer the Math Lab teacher had was wrong, in part, because the question was wrong. No one could answer it correctly. No one could ever earn the word problem button. He felt superior to us children because in all the years he'd given the word problem, no child had ever answered it correctly. I couldn't tell if he thought it was a correct question. Or if he knew the answer was impossible, yet gave it to us deliberately, to demonstrate his superiority while we struggled and, in sixty seconds, failed. As I get older and reflect on the race to answer the word problem, I don't think he understood that the question was impossible; and that his answer, though correct within the reality of his question, was, in fact, incorrect in a real version of reality.

II

Our third grade class voted in the presidential race. Nixon won. While I voted for McGovern, Nixon won. McGovern received three votes in that election: Me, Clarence Joseph, III, and someone else. I remember Clarence Joseph, III holding both hands high in the air above his head each of the three time Miss Todd read McGovern's name. He closed his fists and extended two fingers in a V, a peace sign, on each hand. The next time, and the only other time I remember seeing this image was when Nixon resigned his winnings. I never watched the Watergate hearings on TV during the immeasurable time after school. I do remember, in the end, Nixon held up his fingers in a V with each hand like Clarence Joseph, III. He seemed happy. I don't think the lines at the gas station were long yet. They're all crooks, my mother told me. Or else my step-father. That's why I don't vote. No one ever wins by a single vote. My candidate never wins. Neither candidate would do. I never saw Clarence Joseph, III after the third grade. His father moved them back home. I didn't knew where home was. He seemed to have enjoyed the after-school hearings. I wonder if his father watched with him. I don't know if he voted for McGovern on his own, or if it was because his father persuaded his vote. I do know that I had never considered voting for a presidential candidate until Clarence Joseph, III campaigned for McGovern in Miss Todd's class. I listened to my classmate's speech and voted. He convinced only two of us. I wonder if he ever ran for an office when he got old enough to run. I ran for Treasure that year and lost. It's the only race I ever voluntarily entered. I remember two things about that race: I lost and I spelled "treasurer" without an r at the end. "R. for Treasure." After that, I never wanted to lead. I didn't want to follow, either. He taught me that.

III

The lowest price in memory is 45 cents per gallon.
I didn't ever consider the 9/10 of a cent then. I still
don't, even though I know it exists. I suppose it adds
up to someone. My mother drove to the gas station and
tried to beat the car next to her. The cars already in
front of us didn't seem to bother her. That is, had she
gotten there earlier, she would have raced to beat them
as well. But she only cared that she beat the car that
arrived about the same time she did. Naturally, the cars
way behind us didn't matter. My friend wondered why
his mother wanted to find the cheapest gas when she
planned to get two dollars' worth of gas. He knew that
she would only pay the two dollars wherever she went,
no matter the price per gallon. But by the time he told
me this in high school he already understood the math.
I don't know why he told me that so many years after
he figured out the math. My mother didn't drive when
the gas tank was full. By the time she had to get more
gas, the price would be higher. When she finally drove,
she aimed to use all the gas in the Bug so she could fill
the tank before the price went up again. People fought
at the pump. Crowds, lines, blood. We didn't live far
from anything. Land separated Edison from everywhere
else in the world. An island surrounded by land. When
we drove to the next town, which we rarely did, we
had to pass cow farms and mustard green fields. I think
Pomodoro tomatoes, too. I was in high school when
I heard of cities that didn't have mustard green fields and

cows between them. We drove to Disneyland, or else, to visit some second cousins in LA. I don't remember the price of gas then. More than 45 cents, but not memorable. El Monte, La Puente, Baldwin Park, etc.— right next to each other. A car crashed into our car. The patrol officer told us that the crash happened on the other side of the middle yellow line in the street, so it wasn't his area. We had to wait for the other district's officer, who told us that while our car was presently on his side, the collision originated on the other side of the middle. The first officer was wrong. Forever after that crash I knew that wide openness didn't separate other cities like it separated mine.

IV

The Edison Unified School District started busing twenty three years after the Supreme Court decided in favor of race and the first busload of White kids entered our middle school. They were not the first White kids I'd ever seen; but they were the first ones I noticed. I must have been blind before. I didn't know if any of them had ever seen me. I don't remember their names. I noticed that none of the smart ones in my classes ultimately went to our high school. I didn't notice their absence. I walked around the football stadium with my friend during a game and recognized one of the White kids from the seventh grade. He didn't recognize me. I guess it was him. He seemed older, different, farther.

He didn't see me at the night game. The lights on the field were bright, and he seemed scared to be at our stadium on the south side. Friday night on the south side. I suspect his parents moved to a house outside the busing lines. A receiver raced up the sideline and tried to score. One of our guys caught him near the end zone. I don't remember if they scored on the next play. I'll bet they won the game. I didn't see the play. I saw the White kid from seventh grade. I'm sure he was watching the game, and not us.

V

I felt like a minority at the integrated university. I'd never been a minority in Edison, even during the busing years the White kids came to our middle school. We only went to their schools for games. The university didn't know I existed. "What's your registration number?" interrupted what I tried to tell the officials. In the end, I graduated. I now wish I'd gone into Comparative Literature. But because I didn't read any other languages, only American English, I was restricted. American English didn't exist as a major. So, I thought about English. I quickly tired of the old, big books. I should have majored in something else. Music. I remembered playing the trumpet in the seventh grade. Jazz could have been my home, but I quit playing that same year. I lost interest in the rhetorical jazz of my university protest days as I got older. One-line protest slogans within a chorus of undergraduate protest. It

was a time of apartheid: "It's our money. Divest Now."
Or something like that. No one protested in the rain.
Not during exams. We had some fantastic displays of
protest after midterms, when the weather was nice. I
don't know if anyone saw me at the university protests.
I stopped going because I thought we'd won. I didn't
understand then that we could not win. I read Ellison's
"winner take nothing" in an Afro-American Literature
class the next semester. I wondered if it applied to me.
Anyway, I didn't know what the prize was. But I knew
I didn't win. I didn't know who or what I was racing
against. The university ended in a fast jazz trio that
slows at the end and ends long, longer than the middle.
The individual notes are clear at the end. If I hear the
song again, I can hear the fast middle of the song better
because I remember the ending from before.

VI

The first book I'd ever read was in the second semester
of the eleventh grade. I took five years of math in four
years of high school. That's not because of winning
the math races in elementary school, but because my
Filipino friend's parents told him he should go to
medical school if he didn't want to pick asparagus like
them which forced him to take an extra year of math in
the tenth grade so that he'd reach calculus as a senior in
high school. Because I took the same classes, I reached
calculus, too. He didn't go to medical school. I think
he does something with computers. I'm not sure. I lost

him when we went to different universities. It's the math that my high school teachers noticed. No one realized I hadn't read a book by the eleventh grade. One teacher apologized to me on behalf of his profession because I'd gotten so far without reading. No one required me to read. Neither did I think it was a good idea. I didn't advise myself well in those days of trumpets and footballs, of protest calculus. I didn't understand the apologia. Nor did I get the sense that his profession authorized him to speak for them. Now I read books without being required by anyone. The university texts taught me that the I.Q. test I took in the third grade was culturally biased. Or else, racially biased. (I forget which.) Is a high score on an invalid test invalid? I remember the White psychologist timing me in the third grade. I'd just come from a math race and listened to the air conditioner in the near-silent room with the White man. My skin was hot from the race between the Math Lab and the I.Q. test. I listened to the air conditioner and felt my skin cool down. I don't know how long I listened to the air conditioner noticing the hum, the rhythm, the cool air rhythm we didn't have at home. I heard the tick-tick of the White district psychologist's stop-watch as he waited for me to put pieces of a simple big puzzle together. I realized my score depended on his time.

VII

I didn't know that Whites and Jews were not the same until the third year of graduate school when I talked with one. I didn't know which. Naturally, I talked with other Whites before in official, formal, hierarchical words. But never as people: free minds. Not until our third year. The Jewish man told me that it's not just another White religion. I'm not sure why I was interested. I talked with my White roommate about something unmemorable, the way I would talk with anyone else who didn't force me to consider whether my mind was as free as his, and released an epiphany that would last the entire third year. I don't understand how I lived so long in America without talking with one of them. And without one of them talking with me. This price is high. I repress this. I met an elite Mexican, too, that year. We had no historical reason for becoming friends. Nothing in common—he was from Mexico, immigrated here, spoke Spanish, was Catholic.... And I came to America from central California, spoke no Spanish, believed in nothing, like Thomas the twin, until I could prove it. But more than this, he had servants in Mexico. I considered that my peasant family would have served his rich one in another version of time. A retiming, then. Two realities in a Venn diagram that intersect in time for only part of the two circles, where they are one. We both read Russian novels. Another graduate student invited us to lunch on the last day of a seminar on Time. Let's eat Cuban food, he suggested the way someone suggests when they will pay, and awaited our consent the way people consent when they are not paying. You guys should feel right at home. I asked what Cubans ate. He thought that I should know this as a Mexican. Black Beans, he said. I don't remember how long the instant lasted in my mind as my brain declined to accept black beans. I smelled the eternal pot of pinto beans of my childhood burning.

VIII

I got a part-time job at the Department of Race. I showed aptitude even as a high school student, but gained clarity of race at the university. It was during the tenth grade, the year of two math classes, when I enrolled in the class on race and learned about class. Class race class color race gender class race. The fog is thick in the Edison morning: suspended coalesced water where I worked my first job as a part-time race intern in the Department of Race. I walked to the building in the fog. I grabbed a handful as I walked to the building that rested near my home, coincidently, so I didn't need to catch a bus where I would have trouble seeing my street in time to ring the bell so the bus driver would know to stop and let me off so I could walk from the bus stop to the Department of Race on my first day as a race intern. I walked in the fog. I couldn't see the building even as I knew I approached it on time that first morning. I knew it was there. I walked into the parking lot where I still could not see the Department of Race. I saw no one. I got closer, closer, I walked in the parking lot and saw the behemoth approaching me. I saw the white guys in front. They darkened as I got closer. I watched the Miss

America Beauty Pageant that first night after working as an expert intern in race. We still had a black and white television set when I watched the first two Black Miss Americans among the five finalists. But when I looked at the two out of five Black women mixed with three out of five White women, I could not tell which two were Black and which three were White because they all looked white on our black and white television set. The final two were Black, which clarified things, though I still couldn't see black. The emcee assured us that America would have her first Black Miss. One would be the winner. I had to believe the emcee. Take his word. The winner was Black.

IX

The analogy of investments the banker gave me had to do with changing lanes on the freeway to get into a faster lane. She explained that one investment might not look as good as the next. But, like on the freeway, if I change lanes, time also changes. The new lane might slow down while my old lane speeds up. The lane you just left speeds up. She didn't tell me that sometimes the cars on the freeway go backward. But cars on the freeway don't go backward. I retimed my investment. I got a new advisor.

X

My wife and I had a baby: Miles is the name I chose. Chose it before he was born. She didn't actually agree, but wanted to wait until the delivery. I don't know why, but she didn't want to know the gender. But the baby was a girl. Miles didn't seem right for a girl. Then we chose my wife's last name as our baby's first. With a Mexican father and a Black mother, our baby has blonde hair and green eyes. She defies definition. The lineage on my wife's side: blonde, green-eyed slaves in Canton, Mississippi. Our baby can pass for white in our professional, planned neighborhood. We hope she doesn't want to. Where will she fit in at elementary school? No math races. We're saving for private university tuition. We'll teach her at home to protect her against the lessons she'll learn at school where dead Mayans dead Incas dead Aztecs dead Mexicans dead slaves all die in the first paragraphs. Her I.Q. can't be measured and assigned to any race's bell curve. My baby's a toddler now, but I suspect she's smarter than me. She races through sounds, numbers, letters, colors. She'll speak groups of American words. Then write them.

XI

Books. I read the first story in Borges' collection, *Ficciones*. I hoped the rest wouldn't be as impossible. I skipped through the Table of Contents and found the troubling one: "Pierre Menard, Author of Don Quixote." I wasn't certain at the time, but I didn't think Menard was the original author. I read through this labyrinth and into a connecting one with other writers of Spanish in English translation. They all seemed to lead to one person: an invisible man who is not insane. Music plays in the distance. Sounds race through my Californian mind.

Rosa Darling's Short Story

I wrote a short story about Rosa Darling. She is half Filipino. Her father, whom she never knew, lived in Edison for most of the years she grew up. His parents (his mother, I think) lived at the Filipino Center downtown. Rosa Darling knew them; spent a little time with them on and off. (She had a stepfather whom she considers her father, while we all know, genetically speaking, he is not. All right.) Many years later, when she was already divorced and her daughter was about twelve or thirteen, Rosa Darling thought she should find this father she'd never met so he could know he has a granddaughter, so that she can know her grandfather, and, even more than this, so that Rosa Darling, herself, could have some sort of affiliation with her father. Easily, she found that he lived in San Clemente with his wife and other children. She contacted him by phone and arranged for them to meet in San Clemente. Rosa Darling drove down from Edison with her daughter. They met him. He listened. Spoke a little. And then told her he wasn't interested in an affiliation with either her or his granddaughter. She paid for her portion of the lunch. She drove back to Edison from San Clemente with her daughter and without any hope for the past.

I decided this might make a good short story. However, I then thought this might make an even better stage drama. Perhaps in one Act, like *Doubt: A Parable*. As I listened to her narration, the story seemed, at first, to play as a tragedy, destined to the end. But I decided to write it as a short story because the form of the story, destined to the end, seemed a cleaner prose that could decline both bulk and complexity, and words, for that matter, without skimping on matter without dialogue and pure acting. In addition, I don't know how to write a play. I did think a novel might work, but wondered what I might add to the stealth narrative that could only suffer from unnecessary words. These sorts of stories exist, I'm sure, as I am currently writing a long novel about *work* that includes necessary bulk. But Rosa Darling's short story would have suffered with even one more word.

Exactitude, as Faulkner advises for the short story, harnessed my proclivity to narrate away from the theme, even if I promised to return. But I'm thankful, as I can imagine I might have written either a more robust, offensive prose, or worse, a thick novel that perseverated on absent fathers and shibboleth. Finding a father was the new idea for us. We all knew our fathers, but were ignored by them. That is, they weren't lost, needing to be found. I'd seen my own father, coincidently, at least four times roaming around Edison, not looking for me. So, when Rosa Darling told me she knew her father's parents, knew of her father, and wanted to find him in San Clemente, I became intrigued, personally, as a narrator, because I'd never considered a journey that ends in finding a father. Never considered what I might think on a long drive to, say, San Clemente. Or to the place where he and I might meet for lunch so that I could tell him that I'm interested in an affiliation as a son, and in a grandfather for my daughter, who was yet to be born. *How* a narrator might take this foreign, nearly actual, narrative and construe it into a fiction, as I said, intrigued me. I was not afraid of my father. I wasn't interested in him meeting my daughter, if I'd had one. More to the point, I could not imagine such a narrative. As she spoke, the drama in one act raised its curtain. Since I'm no dramatist, but a short story narrator, I declined the narrative as play, even if it might be a superior stream, and exacted it, perhaps, into a contrived clarification that only thinly veils my proclivity.

I began listening as a narrator, not a writer. The ending concerned me, however. Even as she narrated the actual chronology, I'd leapt ahead and concluded that her father would accept her offer; that she was making the bigger movement. But when he declined in her narrative, I recognized this as a new direction in what would have been common in my writing before: ending the narration with acceptance and unnatural hope. I saw new possibility for the old story: child finds parent and affiliation is declined, with more endings possible. But how does a narrative end when the parent declines the child again? (I should distinguish between mothers and fathers, here, however, because absent mothers, which I cover in another text, is already more interesting than absent fathers. I'm not talking about adoption stories, here, but about children who know their parents, even in absence.) What becomes of the granddaughter? Why did he decline his daughter again? Was it just that his wife and his other children would be disrupted by his denied again daughter and her own newly denied daughter? This is probably the answer. But he'd declined her as an infant. And every Christmas and birthday since then. Even as his parents included her in their existence, he did not. This preceded his new wife and their new children. Then, this is probably not the answer. The reason one human denies the other two discrete times, and the contiguous time between, which is impossible to measure, is not disruption. To deny her a third discrete time in contiguous time is not possible. The ending needed a narrator more than I'd initially suspected as Rosa Darling told me about her drive back from San Clemente.

Afraid. When she drove there. When she walked in. When she thought of coordinating the trip to San Clemente even before she left. But not when she returned from San Clemente. Afraid wasn't it anymore. The worst thing did not happen, as she'd imagined it. Rather, afraid was neutralized. Something eternally worse remained: insignificance.

She paid for her lunch and her daughter's lunch. He offered to pay for the three of them, but she declined. Not for sale. She did not pay for him; but for herself and her daughter. Not exact, to the penny, to two decimal places, but approximately the amount for her and hers. Not his. She didn't calculate the precise amount, but paid precisely. Not to make a point to him that she could not be purchased for the price of two lunches. Not to make a point of showing her daughter how she would and would not allow the world to treat her. Not to make a point that she would not pay for him. She reached into her purse in insignificance and paid the amount that was right.

Her daughter is a singer. Music filled the car as they drove away from San Clemente back to Edison. Her daughter began singing in the car when they had already been on the freeway long enough for San Clemente to be far behind them. Rosa Darling was unaware of the distinction between the silence in her mind and her daughters song. Not because her daughter sang with a jazz singer's timing, but because the distinction was not significant.

My own insignificance isn't something I'd ever considered. Neither did I simply reach for it as an instrument when I wrote Rosa Darling's short story. This distinction must be made, even if tautology has its place. Because my mother suffered from autolalia late in life, I was afraid I might become an autolalic, so persisted in the short story when it wasn't crazy. But this is not why I thought brevity would be successful.

A jazz singer sings and sings the same thing again in the same song and in different songs in the collection. I don't sing. He tried to pay for the three of them. She paid for herself and her daughter. Being half Filipino in California wasn't remarkable. Her daughter, I suppose, if we were to calculate humanity this way, might be considered a quarter. But I think her own father had some Filipino in him; so she would have been more, closer to half. This is something they might have talked about, but did not, I don't think. She didn't live in the Filipino Center, but in a house with her mother and stepfather.

I didn't ask her why, then, when she was already married and divorced with a twelve or thirteen year old daughter, she wanted to meet him. The risk was high, though, I don't think she calculated all the possibilities. She was prepared to hear his side. To tell her side. To start the ending. But she was not prepared for insignificance, entirely. Even her daughter was safe, as she went along without any desire for affiliation of her own, but to drive with her mother and sing along when she conjured the lyrics. And the time. The stereo played and she sang along. Rosa Darling didn't consider the difference. *I'm as restless as a willow in a windstorm. I'm as jumpy as a puppet on a string. I'd say that I had spring fever, but I know it isn't spring. I'm starry eyed, vaguely discontented, like a nightingale without a song to sing.*

He was not as thin as she'd imagined. Not as tall, either. They arranged to meet in a small place near the beach where they could sit outside under the cover overlooking the ocean. She got to San Clemente before their scheduled meeting and drove along the neighborhood streets dead-ending at the beach where she parked and walked in the sand. Hot soles claimed her attention away from her impending meeting with her father who left her forever once. Time appeared. She drove to the place where she would pay for two lunches and learn that her father did not consider her before she drove back home to Edison and listened either to her stereo or her daughter singing a Sarah Vaughan song. She wasn't certain, as she didn't need to distinguish them. I wrote her short story attempting to leave myself out, entirely, which I think I did.

I met my father who was not my father in a place of no time near the water where I heard jazz notes timed and retimed with beats of present where I could land and catch my breath without a father I did not need and did not claim and was not claimed. I did not go for an affiliation or for insignificance but to relieve the doubt about my existence, not my worth, which was nothing to him when I saw him and when he saw me and my daughter who was either born or not born, repeatedly. We do not play with fathers in my family. Daddy, watch this, is something I've never said. Daddy, watch this. I don't hate him. I don't. I'd have to exist as more than a narrator. *I keep wishing I was somewhere else, walking down a strange new street. Hearing words that I had never heard from a man I've yet to meet.*

New Inquisition

Burn the books. That's what he thought. After carrying the old books in his uncle's Army duffle bag from California, he became his own inquisitor because he believed his books influenced his thoughts beyond reality, and, in the end, could only preclude his existence. He hoped to exist after the fire. So, the morning of the night my mother was to die from a ruptured blood vessel in her brain, my absurd second cousin decided to burn the books.

In the basement of my parents' house, where he lived the summer after his first year at the School of Journalism, my absurd second cousin lifted his uncle from California's Army duffle bag, which had his uncle's surname, Espejo, written in heavy black permanent ink on its side so that anyone able to see could see it. He shook the bag of books until they all fell into a pile on the basement floor beneath the window that was at the level of the earth, his only source of light. One hundred books.

He opened the window.

The books climbed into a pile that was, at once, anachronistic and unrecognizable. He tried to separate them into distinct piles that would allow him to investigate properly those books that he wanted to keep. But he instantly recognized the problem: some of the books belonged in more than one pile. The first was a medieval pile. A Spanish in translation pile. An English pile. A metaphysical pile. An American pile. And a grammarian pile. He developed, then, a New Index of Forbidden Books, so that he could burn them with forethought and accuracy.

Once separated, my absurd second cousin picked up one book after another with reference to neither their publication dates nor their piles. He mixed them into an eternal anachronistic instant in his head, which, I suppose, was the very reason he began the inquisition of his mind.

He charged each book with accusations of unreality and, in an effort of fairness, read a sampling of pages, including the notes he had written in their margins. He looked for any redeeming lines in the prose or in his own ramblings that could, objectively, rescue them from execution. Though he took no oath, he understood this process to be an obligation of ontology.

He didn't know with which pile of books to begin. He reached for the biggest one. Big books offended him most because they were too heavy to carry in his bag. It wasn't the closest one, but he reached for the *Condensed Dictionary of English Words*. This would be the first out the window because of its offensive size. From the same pile, the English pile, he grabbed the *Handbook of Words* which he thought would be a good companion for the *Condensed Big Book* as they burned to ashes. Of all the books he threw up to the earth, these were the only two he didn't open before throwing them out.

In order to preserve the anachronicity, he took from another pile. A short story collection from the Spanish in translation pile. Though he remained a follower of Cortazar's trickery, one of the stories, which he'd underlined in red, confused him to the point that he could not decipher in the story the distinction between past and present. By the end of the short story, my absurd second cousin was convinced that no such distinction exists. This book went flying. And because he could not decipher the brief excerpts of Sanskrit that had been omitted from his translation of *One Hundred Years of Solitude*, that book flew.

The first book he'd ever read, *To Kill a Mockingbird*, had none of the marginal writings he wrote in later books. Rather than reread it in order to write his own thoughts in the margins, he threw it out clean. Along with *Native Son* because he thought Bigger had used linguistic devices inferior to his narrative capacity in Book One of that novel. A collection of Brodsky's essays because he worried he couldn't understand the poet's prose while neglecting his poetics. *Song of Solomon*—not because he disagreed with the author, but because he'd always wanted to read it from the first-person unreliable narrator's point of view of the past. He threw out Garcia, an unknown oblique author of bits, essays, cracks, tell-tales, and "insights." *The Pocket Aristotle, The Essential Augustine*, and *From Plato to Nietzsche*, all flew out of his hands, without his attention, as he thought about keeping them. He decided to keep one philosophical text—really a mere essay, *The Myth of Sisyphus*. He kept it because, while in the middle of the book, once, he thought he recognized the narrator's face. Naturally, he threw out all books on how to write: *Simple and Direct*, which he read with the memory of Borges yet to be formed; the thin book, *A New History of the World, Pt. 4*; the *Light Encyclopedia of Poetics*; and *Argument*.

The remaining piles of books presented my absurd second cousin with torment. Though he wanted to burn them all, which he could have done without even creating distinct piles, and, especially, without charging each book individually, he sat next to the remains of his piles and considered the present without them.

He found an old edition of a medical textbook in the basement. Dad told him he could keep it because the advances in medicine rendered the book useless. But my absurd second cousin didn't believe medicine had advanced in the area of life. In the end, he declined to believe that a medical text could decipher life as clearly as the other books in his uncle from California's Army duffel bag. Though he thought about keeping the medical text because he didn't trust physicians, he eventually decided to throw it into the outside pile because he couldn't understand the goal of modern medicine.

An old notebook that contained the beginnings of some of the stories he started writing. Some of the stories only had middles. Only one had an end. He threw this into the pile of forbidden books because it was not a book; and because he planned to start a new collection that was to start with the fire of this pile of books.

And other books I will not mention here. If I mention them all, certainly I will omit books that should have been in his bag. Like the big Russian novels that influenced his thinking more than any other because he studied them the same way he studied mirrors. And Gogol's thin collection because he emphasized the events of a man whose nose was either lost or stolen with the clarity of unreality.

He almost kept some: *Part of The Entire Collected Works of D.H. Lawrence* because his version contained the unfinished essay, "Poetry of the Present." He planned to read it again and finish it himself. And a small volume edited by someone who collected only those stories by Kafka that dealt with reality. A copy of the original *Index of Forbidden Books* (1559).

He kept four books:

1. The 124 page novel, *Pedro Paramo*. The brevity of this big book, along with its companion, provoked him more than any other.
2. Two copies of Ellison's *Invisible Man*. He had filled this book with his marginal ramblings in different colors of ink, starting with red, so that he could

easily identify during which reading his thoughts progressed, and during which they decayed. He read this book every three years, each time retrieving new meanings of existence. The second copy of this book contained none of his ramblings—he kept it clean, wrapped in plastic next to the collection of Morrison books.

3. Naturally, he kept Borges. The second volume of Borges' only collection to have been lost without traces. My absurd second cousin discovered the only original version of "The Garden of Forking Paths" where the blind man had playfully written the word "reality" where he ultimately wrote the word "time" for an undetermined and poorly understood reason. In this edition, there was a footnote near the end admitting that the words may be switched here, and in other stories. This was not, however, the volume which contained the manifesto that big books are offensive both to the reader and the writer. That volume may have already been recovered. Nor did it contain part three of his refutation of time. That volume has not been recovered.

At the bottom of the pile of Russian books in translation, he found one poem by Brodsky he decided to keep. This poem, however, was originally written in English, an should have been in the American pile.

By the end of this short story, except for these four, plus the poem, my absurd second cousin will have thrown his books into the light where they formed a pile of forbidden books on the earth above my parents' basement. Ma heard the noise of flying books landing in a pile outside her kitchen window and looked down to see from where the books originated. She opened the back door and saw the pile of forbidden books.

He walked up the stairs with matches and a bottle of Ma's rubbing alcohol that I used to rub her feet since the year they lost their feeling because of her diabetes. Walked through the kitchen and through the back door where he found Ma standing in front of the books.

Move. I'm going to burn them.

Not in my yard. Not with my rubbing alcohol.

Move.

No.

I'm done carrying these books with me. I put them in my uncle's Army duffle bag in California and flew into Chicago with them. I've read parts of most of them. They are swirling in my mind and have me confused about reality. I don't appear to exist without them.

What do you mean you don't exist? You're my twin, Tomas the twin's, grandson. I'm blind from diabetes, but I can see you. You are not alone in the world, absolute, like you've convinced Mimi. You're a man in my family, like the others. Now give me my rubbing alcohol. I'm going inside. Your words of existence are giving me a headache.

MAN IN OIL

I went to a foreign city to mourn. Since I had never been
to New York, never even considered it as a Californian
with no ties to the east, I decided to go. In the end, I
narrowed my trip to Paris, Florence, and New York.
New York, then—since I only speak English. I wanted
to see a play in a New York theater. But when I arrived,
I found that there was no theater in New York on
Monday. Dark Mondays.

I walked into Greenwich Village on the dark
Monday afternoon. It's a clever place: architecture firms,
shoe stores, apartments, European coffees in white and
black stores, art galleries.

I went to Soho. Italian lemon ice. Look at the facades.
I made a few haphazard turns during the walk and found
myself on a little street headed back to the subway. I
walked into a small art gallery I'd missed earlier. I didn't
know if I'd walked passed it before or if I'd turned up
a different street. Or, if it appeared different traveling
back in the opposite direction. The gallery interested

me from the outside, so I went in to get relief from the summer rain. I walked around the place and looked at some of the paintings I didn't find interesting. (There weren't many on the walls; and I didn't recognize any of the painters. So mine was nothing more than a cursory look—not really an investigation of art.) Only two or three got my attention. One, especially, on the back wall.

I looked at the words printed on a card next to the painting to get some insight, but there was nothing there for me. So I looked back at the painting. It was an oil of a man in a casket with his eyes open. A dead man in a dark suit: black hair, black mustache, black casket. He wore a white shirt. And the rest of the painting was blue like the sky the other day in California. Maybe there were some clouds—I don't remember. I do remember that the dead man's eyes were open. A sort of light-brown. Not very dead-looking at all. They seemed to notice something.

The unctuous curator, who had been busy with real customers, walked toward me along the wall in the back of his gallery as I looked at the man in oil. I watched his face as he walked back. I didn't recognize it. He started talking before he was directly in front of me: I'm glad you finally made it in. I've been expecting you. I didn't think you were coming at all, Sir.

I looked around and didn't see anyone else in this part of the gallery. He must have been talking to me. Must have been expecting me. Me? I looked behind and only saw the man in oil. Yes, then, he must have been talking to me.

I stared at the man's face. He appeared familiar. Distant, but familiar. I sensed I recognized him from somewhere in the past. I couldn't say from where. Either from a few days or a week ago. Or from a long, indeterminable time ago. I couldn't really remember any details about the man. Only that I recognized him vaguely.

What could I do? I smiled. Before I had much of an opportunity to speak, the unctuous curator asked, Did you have a tough time finding my place?

In fact I hadn't. That is, I wasn't looking for his place—and was certain I would never look for it again once I left—so, No, I did not, I said.

Good then. Glad to hear it, Sir. I see you've already found the oil.

I stood back from the wall and looked at the man in the casket. I tried again from the side. Up close. Farther. A blurred recognition. Someone famous from the past? An artist I should know? A distant relative? Someone I'd met once or twice in my line of work? I looked again at the painter's name for a clue, but saw that I had never heard of him before. I don't remember his name now. I asked the unctuous curator to tell me about the artist.

He smiled. Smiled then laughed as if I were simply playing with him. Making a small witticism. You've always had that dry wit, Sir. We both looked back at the man in oil. The details of his face seemed alive. I could see a sort of expression in his face. An emotion, or else a thought. The dead man seemed pensive. Looking at something. Or *for* something. I stared at his face.

Just what you're looking for, Sir. I thought of you as soon as I got the piece in.

His words were absurd. But, somehow, I got the feeling he was right. This seemed to be my oil. Mine, alone. I didn't know why. And, now, I don't care to know.

Would you like me to arrange to have the oil sent to your home in California?

With a little edge to my voice, I asked, Have we met before? How did he know where I lived?

He laughed again. Some real customers had entered the gallery a few minutes earlier. As he walked toward the apparent tourists, laughing, the unctuous curator looked back at me and said, I'll take care of it for you, Sir. Love the wit.

I turned to walk out of the Soho art gallery. I passed the unctuous curator and said goodbye. He looked at me and again said, I'll take care of the oil for you, Sir. I hope to see you on your next trip. He waved.

I left.

Several weeks passed before the Man In Oil arrived in California.

I stared at the viscous oil of the dead man in the casket with his eyes still noticing. Then his face seemed without expression or emotion. No pensive squint. No sadness in his eyes. No longing. No smirk. No noticing. No more.

I didn't recognize him at all. This was an absurd oil.

I placed it on a back wall in my house in search of the familiarity I sensed in the Soho art gallery. I had no memory of the man. No sense that I knew him from before. No relative. No ancestor from antiquity. No vague acquaintance. Never met him before. He didn't look like anyone I knew. He didn't even look like a real human. The man in oil didn't exist in the past. I am certain of this: the man exists only in the present.

The Man In Oil is here in my California home along a wall in the back for everyone to see.

LOVE CHILD

I was conceived in the spring, I imagine. Of course, I
don't remember any of that, though I've heard from my
mother again and again. She named me after the actor in
the movie she watched during labor. An unknown actor
whose movies I've never seen, though I should probably
watch one or two to see where I come from. This is
not a story about a lost father or a lost son. Neither
is it a story about a found father, because no one is
looking for him. Anyway, he's dead. What becomes of a
child who does not know his dead father? I read a story
about such an incident. Well, it was more a novella
from Mexico: *Pedro Paramo*. I'd always avoided father-
son stories for the obvious reason: I wasn't interested.
Even when I became a father, I remained disinterested
in such stories, entirely. But this one about a dead
Mexican father and his son's search for what belongs
to him interested me. I tried to tell myself that I was
only interested in it for literary reasons. The content, I
protested, was meaningful only insofar as Rulfo needed

some substance to get these dead characters talking. I didn't protest to anyone in particular.

I met a professor of Spanish Literature at a dinner party a few years ago and asked if I could schedule a meeting with him in his office one afternoon to discuss the novella. The professor agreed. I only have one question, I said. I don't understand the book.

The Spanish Lit professor laughed and said, No one can understand that guy! He has dead people talking to each other in the grave.

I confessed he'd provided me with great relief. I've been tormented, especially at night, when thinking about how a dead young man might narrate a novella. Just as I thought about simply accepting this as an artistic Mexican narrative device. I stumbled as I recalled that the narrator started out the novella alive and died somewhere in the middle pages of the barren earth.

My city is brown, with green accents along the levee where I jog after work. During the summers, the heat couples with the water and attracts insects that hover more than fly near the edge of the slough where the jogging trail traces the edge. While the beginning is elevated, the trail quickly descends to below the levee, at the water's level. So, underground, if not under water. I see docked boats at the beginning. Jet skis in the middle. And ducks at the end—where I turn around and run back to the beginning boats. The insects usually adjust their cloud to encompass me as I try to avoid them. I cannot be sure which of us bothers the other more. I run along the slough that had water in prior centuries. Now it's dry. Sometimes I run on the trail that traverses along the edge, where the water once touched the land, while other times I run down into the dry slough below the ground. Rocks, some weeds, and a brown dust are there beneath my running shoes. I'd prefer to run in the early morning if I could. Rather, I run in the evenings when I get home from work in an office. I need the day to progress before my bones are ready to run. In any case, I try to stay in shape.

I take time in the mornings to work on a novel I've been writing for years. I made some notes that I continually expand. Some sections are already written; others are still notes I must convert into prose. I find I can work best in the basement where even the light of day cannot penetrate. I use some lamps that provide me with a sense of night, when I believe I think best, while still morning, when I know I think best. These notes for a novel only have meaning to me, I imagine. Naturally, some of the characters are dead. But while I ran at the bottom of the slough last evening I decided that whether some characters are dead is immaterial. What matters is that my narrators are alive.

LINE JUDGE

I began playing tennis in the summer after the third grade after I'd seen a Scandinavian player on television. I watched the Sunday event for five hours. My mother took us to K-Mart that evening for some unrelated items. In the Sport section of the impressive and bright department store I found a tennis racket made of wood and string that appeared like the virtual one I'd seen on television earlier that the day. I believe the price marked was $3.99. I then picked up three unpressurized tennis balls in a plastic bag stapled at the top. This was during summer vacation before the fourth grade was to begin. I went to the park and played tennis against the beige handball wall near the courts. I played this way for more than an hour, but less than five, as I recall, during the height of the sun. For eleven days I hit the poor balls against the beige handball wall with forehands only, then backhands only, then serves that, to my mind, mimicked the precise motions I'd seen on television for five hours. As the years continued, I joined a summer tennis team early in my adolescence, and was the sixth-ranked player on the six-member team. I played doubles with the first-ranked player and improved in both doubles and singles. In the end, I don't remember my record, but do remember both winning and losing.

I continued playing tennis informally at the park with a dedicated tennis club house. While I never entered any tournaments after that initial season, I was a real fan. After I'd become a man, I joined the staff at the tennis club and, sometimes, worked as a chair umpire for the children's tournament. With time, I began to umpire the seniors. Then the regular adults. This was not at all difficult, as the players were generally trusting of each call and each no call. Oh, there was an occasional dispute, but I believe I handled things fairly, and was able to keep the match moving. If I ever had real doubt, I could always ask the players to play a let, which didn't always satisfy each player, but did approximate fairness, which seemed to be what the two sides craved even more than winning. Certainly, since no money or fame was involved, all that remained was a sense of achievement on the court. And fairness.

My style of judging seemed to coincide well with the tenor of our club. And with the sport, itself, I'd imagined. Regional tournament directors invited me to join their team of umpires and line judges at bigger tournaments. Because this intimidated me, a simple chair umpire for a small club, I accepted the invitation, but asked to be placed on a line, and not in the chair. Since so many other umpires wanted the big position, high above the court, where they could hold more power, tournament directors were delighted to leave the lines to me.

I rotated between the service line, middle service line, the side line, and the baseline. I did not mind the middle service line because I only had to judge the initial serve. If the serve remained inside the lines, the play continued, leaving me free to disregard the rest of the point. The service line judge, who judged the depth of the serve, too, could rest once the ball was in play. The side service line judge, however, needed to judge the serve and the subsequent shots, as he would also judge whether the ball remained inside the sideline during the rest of the point. The baseline judge, however, needed to remain vigilant throughout the entire point once it began.

I enjoyed the baseline more than the rest. As my career burgeoned, I became known within my sphere as a keen baseline judge. I continued to be invited to bigger and bigger tournaments. Being a line judge was never a goal of mine; but I continued climbing the ranks of the tennis circuit. In fact, I became a line judge at a national tournament which attracted many of the top players. Even the top players. Well, all right, the number one-ranked player in the world. During one of the matches that did not include him, but two lesser-ranked players on a remote court during the one of the biggest national tournaments of my time, I was the baseline judge. Deep in the third set I did not make a call on a ball that landed on the outside part of the baseline. The highly-ranked player on my side of the court was unable to reach the ball and lost the point. As he ran toward the ball, in my direction, he leaned to reach it, but missed. His momentum carried his nose near the part of the line that the ball hit. He rose from his run, still headed in my direction, and shouted directly at me, and, at once, the world, Out!

I stared ahead, vacantly. Line judges are taught not to engage an enraged tennis player. He continued to shout. But this was now directed at me, only, and not the world. Obscenities. Spit. Volume. Red. He turned to the Chair Umpire who, without the benefit of video cameras or digital trackers on the remote court, was unable to see the ball land as the player, himself, running to reach the ball on the line, blocked the Chair's view. The Chair listened, explained that I'd had the cleanest view—perhaps second only to the running player in dispute—and that he could not overrule my call without clear evidence that I was wrong. My call stood as the most reliable, fairest call in this game of lines and judgment, with all its faults.

After more back and forth between the highly-ranked player and the Chair high above the court, my call stood. Even as the highly-ranked player walked back to our side of the court, he stared directly at me as if to document his superiority as a man, even though he was unsuccessful at changing my call. And even if he was unsuccessful at making me feel, in any way, inferior to him as a man. Nevertheless, he stared down at me sitting in my chair as his walk drifted toward the correct part of the court so that play could resume.

He served. As the rest of the points continued throughout that particular game, he shot stares at me. Even words, which I won't repeat here, as they were directed at me in a volume that only I could hear, along with a few fans sitting behind me. For the next two sets, leading into the fifth, the highly ranked player shot stares at me. I suspect that's because the momentum of the match shifted and our highly-ranked player began to flounder the instant I made the call that stood the test of his spirited grievance. Also, in part, because the other highly-ranked player began swinging with good fortune causing the match to matriculate into a deciding fifth set. All the while, I sensed the enraged player blamed me for his decline from what appeared to be certain victory when I made my call. That is, when I called balls out, even if he agreed, he shot irate stares of ironic disbelief, let's say, that I got one right. When a ball was clearly within the boundaries of play, and I made no call, as was appropriate, he shouted, At least you got one right! And so on, as the highly-ranked player continued to decline, coming closer and closer to losing the match.

In fact, this was to be the last point. He was serving, and had missed the first serve into the net. Of course, he would never fault himself for this serve into the net that was all his fault. No. Neither did he accept blame for missing forehand after forehand, backhand after backhand, balls into the net, way outside the lines so that they could not possibly be questioned, all before I made the call that stood against his protest. Even if I'd made a mistake, which I do not concede, that would be negligible when compared with all the mistakes he made throughout the entire match, including his assault on me, a principled line judge. But as a line judge, it seems, I am allowed no mistakes at all. Perfection is my only choice. Perfection which is to be adjudicated by imperfect people in an imperfect system of judging motion against stillness. Yet, I'm allowed no mistakes. And, perhaps, the final blow, even if I were to be perfect, I must remain silent against attack.

As I stated earlier, he served the first ball of what was to be the final point, handing the other highly-ranked player the win, into the net. Only his second serve stood between him and defeat. He tossed the ball up into the sun and sliced through it with perfect angle, speed, control, and ultimate placement into the service square and ran forward into the court. I shouted, Foot Fault, ending the point, the game, the set, and the match.

I stared straight ahead, and not at the highly ranked player.

Before he could attack me, the Chair spoke into the microphone: Overruled, second service.

Except for me, no one knows whether the highly-ranked player stepped on the line when he served. There were no cameras on this remote court. No other line judge was assigned to the baseline on my side.

The player, himself, was looking into the sun, and not at his feet. Only the Chair could have been watching the highly-ranked player's feet along with me. The precision of the call remains unknown, as the two of us called it differently. But his call stood. Mine did not.

The highly-ranked player picked up the tennis ball, tossed it into the air, and served us both a second opportunity.

1565646

Made in the USA